WHAT A SHOCK

As she waited for the bank switchboard to connect her, the office door opened. Stacy's mouth dropped. In her ear a voice kept saying something like 'May I help you' as Stacy stared at what had to be the handsomest man she had ever seen.

He wasn't movie star handsome. No, he didn't have perfect features, but he was tall, hard muscled, with red hair, a strong, slim face, light eyes, and he was wearing what had to be a custom-tailored suit. That alone was enough to shock the population on Corver Island.

Stacy slowly lowered the receiver into the phone cradle, and asked "Good morning, may I help you?"

Honeymoon House

PHOEBE MATTHEWS

AVON
PUBLISHERS OF BARD, CAMELOT AND DISCUS BOOKS

HONEYMOON HOUSE is an original publication of Avon Books. This work has never before appeared in book form.

AVON BOOKS
A division of
The Hearst Corporation
959 Eighth Avenue
New York, New York 10019

Copyright © 1979 by Diane McClure Jones
Published by arrangement with the author.
Library of Congress Catalog Card Number: 79-54932
ISBN: 0-380-45153-0

First Avon Printing, December, 1979

AVON TRADEMARK REG. U.S. PAT. OFF. AND IN
OTHER COUNTRIES, MARCA REGISTRADA,
HECHO EN U.S.A.

Printed in the U.S.A.

Chapter One

Stacy slowly twisted her head in methodical circles, tracing a pattern with her small pointed chin. To the left shoulder, up toward the ceiling, down to the right shoulder, pulled in tight to the neck, and across to the left shoulder again. A series of popping sounds from the back of her neck followed her head movements.

"Oh, I never thought there would be so much paperwork," she said to the room in general.

Laura mumbled some sort of agreement. The phone rang; Laura lifted the receiver without looking up from the papers on her desk. Then another line lit up, and Laura pushed a button to put it on hold. Stacy started to lift her phone to take the second call, but just then a third call came in. Deciding to answer that one, she picked up her phone and said, "Leitzel–Green Design. Good morning."

"This Leitzel or Green?" a harsh male voice demanded.

"Stacy Green speaking."

"Listen, Stacy Green, I delivered that carpeting six weeks ago, and you promised me payment on delivery. I never should have left it."

"Mr. Davis," Stacy said quickly, her words rushing over each other to drown him out. She had heard his tirades all too often. "I really am sorry, I know we're late on that payment, but I haven't been able to collect one cent on that account yet. I have sent out two billings and made three phone calls, but I'll have to wait another month before I can turn the account over to a collection agency, and I really don't want to do that—"

"I am going to turn you over to a collection agency!" Davis cut in.

"I don't blame you, I really don't, but please Mr. Davis, let me—listen, suppose I pay you half now, I mean right now. I mean, I will put the check in the mail today and then, whether I collect that account or not, I'll pay the balance in thirty days. Okay?"

"No, it is not okay," Davis thundered, "but half is better than nothing." He slammed down his receiver and Stacy rubbed her ear.

Laura Leitzel covered her mouthpiece with her hand and hissed, "Did he buy it?"

Stacy started to answer, but the phone rang again. She nodded yes and grabbed the receiver. "Leitzel-Green Design. Good—"

"That you, Stacy?"

"Yes."

"Tom Barrows here. Listen, I've got the bill here for that paint I used on the Hall place last month and it's already past due. You still owe me two hundred—"

"Oh, Tom, I know, I've been going through the bills this morning, and I'll have that money to you by next month because—"

"Hey, Stace, spare me the sob story, huh? I told you when you opened your business that you'd better figure on losing money for the first year. I know, I've been through it and I sympathize, but listen, hon, I do have to pay for the paint. Just get me the forty bucks for the paint and we'll let my labor charges ride."

"I love you," Stacy said fervently.

"Forty bucks worth?"

"In the morning mail," Stacy promised. She pushed the button to cut off his call and dialed the bank.

"Savings department, please."

As she waited for the bank switchboard to connect her, the office door opened. Stacy's mouth dropped. In her ear a voice kept saying something like 'May I help you?' as Stacy stared at what had to be the handsomest man she had ever seen.

He wasn't movie-star handsome; no, he didn't have perfect features, but he was tall, hard muscled, with red hair, a strong, slim face, light eyes, and he was wearing what had to be a custom-tailored suit. That alone was enough to shock the population on Corver Island.

Stacy slowly lowered the receiver into the phone cradle, and asked, "Good morning, may I help you?"

The man glanced around the office, and Stacy became painfully aware of the confusion in the small room. She and Laura sat behind two cluttered desks. Four file cabinets overflowed with papers, and the one extra wooden chair was filled with Priscilla, the white Persian cat, who often insisted on coming to the office with them. Blueprints and design sketches were stapled crookedly all over the walls.

"I was told by the realtor that you do remodeling projects."

"Yes, indeed, Mr.—?"

"Hamilton. I've bought the old Montgomery place."

"Birch House? Oh yes, I knew it was for sale."

"Then you're familiar with it?"

"I haven't been inside," Stacy admitted. She stood up and walked around the desk to remove Priscilla from the chair. "But I know the property. Would you sit down a minute?"

"No. Can't stay. I have to get the next ferry back to Seattle. And I can tell you in about three seconds what I want, and you can answer me in one second with a yes or a no. I want that place renovated. I've already been to the local contractor—Phillips—know him? Good. He knows about the wiring and plumbing, but I need you to design the renovation, keeping in mind that the place is to be functionally modern but historically correct in appearance."

"Historically? It—that house isn't exactly any period, I mean, it's really early Island and that's about—"

"Fine, do it in early Island, then. But make it right. Use the correct wallpapers, trim, carpets, furniture; I leave it up to you. The house was built in 1896, I'm told, so I want every detail to look as though it existed in 1896."

"You, uh, you want antique rugs and furniture?"

"Right."

"Do you have pieces already that—"

"Nothing, not a doorknob. You find everything. I don't care where. Can you handle it?"

"Yes, but, well, that sort of renovation runs into a lot—I mean, buying antiques means dealing in cash, you see, and—"

"Right. I'll give you this as a starter. When you run out, contact me, and I'll come see what you've done with it. If I'm satisfied we'll go on from there."

He pulled a leather folder from his inside breast pocket, ripped out a check, leaned over Stacy's desk, and filled it in while he talked. "The contractor will take design instructions from you, then contact me directly for estimates and payments so that you don't have to worry about his money. Keep a running account on your expenditures and call me when you hit bottom on this."

"How—how—I mean, uh." Stacy picked up the check and swallowed. Ten thousand dollars. She stared at him, her black eyes wide in her small pixie face. "Mr. Hamilton, could you give me some idea of the price range of furnishings you want? I mean, is this to cover—uh, three rooms, four rooms, the rugs, or what?"

"I said authentic. That's what I want. Birch House was a summer house, right, and that's what it is going to be again. Find me authentic summer house furniture from that period. And rugs, well, the floors are going to be natural wood, aren't they? So—listen!" He broke off abruptly, then exploded, "I'm paying you to figure that out. I haven't time. Do what you can and we'll go from there. The price isn't important as long as I can see where the money went. If you only get halfway across the front hall and I like it, we'll keep going."

"Oh. I see, but, uh, just a minute."

He was already at the door with his hand on the knob and his back to her.

"Mr. Hamilton!"

He turned and glared.

"I don't know, I mean I have to have some idea about—could you at least tell me what textures, styles—"

His frown deepened, and Stacy added quickly, "What's your favorite color? You must have some preference?"

"What's yours?" he shot back.

"Mine? But it is *your* house."

"So put *your* favorite color in *my* house and we'll both be happy. Blast, I'll miss that ferry." And he was gone. The door slammed behind him.

"Well, I never!" Stacy exclaimed.

Laura Leitzel had kept busy at her desk, her head bent over her papers and the phone receiver to her ear while Mr. Hamilton was in the office, but as soon as the door closed, she hung up and stared at Stacy. Her eyebrows rose in her round face.

"What was that all about?"

"We're saved, I think," Stacy said cautiously, then grabbed the phone. "What's John's number down at the realty office?"

Laura rattled it off—she had a phenomenal memory for phone numbers—and Stacy dialed it.

"John? Stacy Green. A Mr. Hamilton was just in here . . . yes, he said you recommended us, thank you kindly, friend, and he left a rather sizeable check. I was wondering . . . you're sure? . . . oh, my gosh! Bless your heart! Thanks again!"

Stacy dropped the receiver into place and stared at the check. Then she let out a whoop and dashed over to Laura.

"Look at that! We can pay the bills, my girl!"

"Ten thousand! I can't believe it. Maybe it'll bounce."

Stacy grinned. "No way. Do you know who Mr. Hamilton, Mr. Avery Hamilton is?"

"No, but I bet you're going to tell me," Laura said.

Stacy spun around on one foot like a ballet dancer and hugged herself in delight. She was a slim woman with a small impish face framed in a close cap of short black hair. Her black eyes were large and heavily fringed with dark lashes so that when she was excited and her eyes widened, they seemed to fill her pale face.

"According to our dear John, Mr. Hamilton is one of *the* Mr. Hamiltons of Hamilton House hotel and motel chains, and he bought the old Birch House as a gift for someone and paid cash for it. When he explained that he wanted it renovated and asked if he should bring in a Seattle firm, our precious John said, 'If you want it authentic, get our local contractor to do the work and our local firm of Green and Leitzel to do the design because they are experts in this sort of thing.' "

Laura let out a whistle.

"Is that all you can say?" Stacy demanded. "You greet salvation with a whistle?"

"I will greet Mr. Hamilton any way you like," Laura said. "Shall I bow when he reappears?"

A slight frown creased Stacy's forehead. "Actually, Mr. Hamilton is the only thing I don't much like about this whole deal. He seemed, well, not very friendly. In fact, he wasn't even very polite."

"I'll take ten thousand instead of courtesy any day," Laura said.

"I know," Stacy agreed. "Mother always said, 'Don't look a gift horse in the mouth.' So I won't. But Mrs. Hall was so hard to work with, and now we are fighting for every penny she owes us, and, well, it would be nice to get a client who is pleasant *and* solvent."

"If you've got to choose," Laura said, "take solvent."

"I suppose I ought to drive on out to Birch House now and look it over. Want to come along?"

"No, I'm trying to track down that drapery material for the dentist's office."

"All right. I think I'll dash off checks for Mr. Davis and Tom and deposit Mr. Hamilton's check in our account."

"That reminds me. If Mr. Windfall Hamilton hadn't arrived, how were you planning to pay Davis? I heard you tell him you would."

"I was just about to wipe out my savings account and then see if I could get a loan on my car," Stacy admitted. "Tell you one thing, Laura. We won't use Davis anymore. He's getting paid in full today and then he's off our list."

Laura's round face dimpled. "Good for you."

Stacy grabbed her car keys and dropped them into her jacket pocket. Without bothering to sit down at her desk, she leaned over the top and wrote out the two checks, then typed the envelopes. Dropping the two envelopes, a deposit slip, and Mr. Hamilton's check into her other pocket, she waved good-bye over her shoulder to Laura and walked down the street to the bank.

A heavy gray sky hung above the small shopping district. Beyond the one street of shops and offices, fir trees rose like dark walls, blocking in the town. A few sea gulls wheeled high above them in the dark sky. The water's edge, which was less than a quarter of a mile away from the main street, was not visible, although Stacy could clearly hear the ferry boat whistle.

After she deposited the check, she dropped the envelope for Mr. Davis into the mailbox. She looked at Tom's envelope, hesitated, then jammed it back into her pocket. No need to mail it. Maybe she could find some more work for him on this Birch House project. If so, she would drop by his place later, give him his check, and see if he were interested. He would be pleased that she was paying him half his bill, not just the forty dollars for the paint, and she knew that he needed the work. Like her, he had started his paint contracting business on nerve and hope, and although he'd been in business three years compared to her one, he was probably still in debt for his truck and equipment.

"Sometimes I think that three-fourths of this island owes everything it owns to the other fourth," Stacy muttered. She cut across the parking lot to the side street where she had parked her car in the morning. Sliding behind the wheel, she dug her keys out of her pocket and inserted one in the ignition. As long as she could pay the office rent and keep the car out of hock she could keep going, but until a half an hour ago, she had been wondering how much longer she could meet her bills. Now a handsome, if rather gruff, miracle named Avery Hamilton had given her a new lease on the future. Whether or not the lease was short term depended on her ability to please him with the renovation plans for Birch House.

As she drove out of town and turned up Sunday Hill, she caught her breath at the familiar but ever exciting view. The sky hung like a drooping gray stage canvas, its darkness mirrored in the cold water. Sea and sky, stretching out from the sharp drop of the hill, were a plain cardboard gray. Across the far horizon, though, spread a ribbon of bright light, a miraculous tear in the cloud cover. In that narrow strip the Olympic mountains shone, distant snow-covered peaks caught in the bright rays of the hidden sun.

The road wound inward toward the island, losing the water view, then branched off to the old Montgomery place, known for years as Birch House for its eight white canoe birches gleaming in a cluster on the front lawn. Stacy parked the car on the side of the road, climbed out, and walked up the old mud driveway. A few remnants of picket fence stuck out from the wild tangle of blackberry bushes that had taken over the yard. If the briar bushes had moved into the house through the windows and filled the rooms, she would not have been surprised. Old Mr. Montgomery had let the place run down badly before his daughter moved him to her own home and put Birch House up for sale. He had not been well enough to care for the place, but Stacy could understand his reasons for hanging on as long as he could. She stopped at the front door, turned and gazed over the long slope of the hill, past the birches and the ever-present stands of fir, to the distant water. The split in the sky had closed and the view was a sheet of gray, moving rain. It would reach her soon.

"It must be a splendid sight from here on a sunny day," she thought, and remembered seeing the old man sitting on the front steps in the sun when she had driven by.

The door was unlocked as John had said it would be. She stepped inside and knew why he didn't worry about locking the place. There was nothing to steal. Wallpaper peeled from the old walls. Paint flaked from the woodwork. If the house once contained valuable lighting fixtures, they had been replaced by ugly modern globes. These disturbances were superficial and Stacy shut them from her mind, concentrating on the size and arrangement of the rooms. First, the entry hall, she thought, and turned slowly to gaze up at the fan window above the door. Who had thought of that? It did not particularly match the architecture, yet it had its own charm. On bright days its pattern would light the opposite wall. The door itself was certainly the original but the hardware had been replaced. She would find authentic hardware. The size of the entry hall would accommodate a bentwood hall tree or perhaps a wardrobe, if she could find a really interesting piece. And a chair. And a carpet. Perhaps a mirror. All right. Mentally she listed the things she would search out.

Furniture would take time to find, but first she must make decisions about kitchen and bathroom fixtures, changes in doorways or cupboards, wall coverings, lighting fixtures. She turned into the parlor and clapped her hands in delight at the fireplace. Around the edges of the rough board that covered its opening, she could see its basic design, fortunately undisturbed except for the paint. That could be removed and the original wood of the mantel refinished. The window proportions were better than she had hoped, opening the room to the distant water view. The room would be too dark for modern tastes, though. She peered out through the narrow side window, noted the bare, gnarled branches of a flowering-cherry tree of considerable age, and knew at once that the window should be replaced with double glass doors, probably French doors, opening onto a patio. To be authentic the patio should be gravel, but perhaps Mr. Hamilton would prefer old brick. She would check with him on that. And on the doors. Perhaps he did not want any architectural changes.

"Hello, Stacy?" a male voice called.

"Tom? Through here!" she shouted.

She smiled to herself as she listened to him tromp through the house. How could a man who could paint window casings without ever spotting the glass be so heavy on his feet?

Tom Barrows filled the parlor doorway with his bulk. He pushed his hat back from his blond hair and grinned.

"How did you know I was here?" Stacy asked.

"Stopped by your office to tell you not to fret about that paint money. I can last another week. So Laura told me you'd had a windfall offer to do this place."

"Look it over with me, Tom. Phillips is doing the remodeling, and I'll tell him you'll do the painting and papering. No waiting here for your pay." She dug into her pocket and pulled out his envelope. "Here, I have this for you now."

"Thanks, Stacy. I appreciate the work. Things are slow."

"Don't I know?" she agreed.

Wandering through the house with Tom deepened Stacy's sense of belonging. She had tried to leave the Island once, hoping to escape the memory of her parents' death and the lonely high school years boarding with her great-aunt. She and Auntie Virginia kept their peace with one another but no real affection existed. She knew the old lady offered her a home through a sense of duty and a need for the room-and-board money paid out of Stacy's parents' estate. After high school Stacy used the balance to attend a junior college north of Seattle, then took a job with a Seattle decorating firm.

At first, she had enjoyed the independence of the rooming house at college and the apartment in the city. But the nights crowded in on her, empty and lonely, and the weekends became unbearable. She contacted old friends, especially Laura who had a small apartment on the Island, and soon she was spending every weekend back on Corver Island.

"Why not move in with me and commute?" Laura asked, and so Stacy did that for a while, riding the ferry to work every day. But finally Stacy left her job when it turned into a dead end. Then Laura quit her job too, and they decided to pool their savings and open their own decorating firm on the Island. As assets they had their lifelong friendships with practically everyone on the Island, and as liabilities they had a lack of funds that would have terrified anyone with a degree of caution.

Tom was one of the assets. And John, who had thrown several jobs their way. And old friends of her parents who gave her small jobs. Her own skill earned her new clients, but some were hard to work with and many were slow to pay.

"This could be our big break," she told Tom. "If I can come up with a smashing room or two, he'll let me do the whole house. He's a little hard to talk to, but I think he wants to spend a great deal of money."

"No limit?"

"There must be, but I don't know what it is yet."

"That sounds risky. I never worked on that kind of basis."

"It's odd, all right. But I'll do what he asked for the first step and then try to pin him down. I think maybe I'll do sketches of a finished product, come up with an estimate, and see if I can corner him into a more definite agreement."

The stairs creaked under Tom's heavy tread. "Four bedrooms up here. Not too large. The one with the adjoining door must have been a nursery."

"Too small," Stacy said, glancing in. "Wonder if he has children?"

"He didn't tell you who would live here?"

"As for that," Stacy said slowly, "he didn't say anyone would live here. I think I should know. If there are children, that front room with the bay window would make a beautiful nursery. The little room could be converted into a master bath and dressing room."

"If he wants it really authentic, we could stick an outhouse in back."

Stacy laughed. "He said something about making it authentic but functional. And that means, make it look old but be sure the plumbing and heating are modern."

She ran her fingers along the balustrade. It was simple, without carving, but when she pressed a fingernail into the old paint she could tell that beneath the peeled layers was hardwood that could be refinished.

"What about the floors, Tom?"

He knelt and ran his fingers across them. "I'll be darned. Cedar. Splinters are wicked, but if I can get a good hard surface on it, the color should be fantastic."

"You want to do the floors?"

"Was Phillips planning to?"

"He hates messing with anything that isn't construction. I'll tell him you'll do all the interior finishes if you like. Want the outside paint job?"

"Whatever you can throw my way, Stacy."

"I'd rather work with you than anyone," Stacy said truthfully. "I know I can count on you. Of course, I could be off this job in a month, but I'm sure that once you start, Phillips will keep you on. So you should get the whole job even if I don't."

"You will," Tom said, sounding confident.

Stacy followed Tom downstairs to the kitchen. She had left it until last because she had an overwhelming love for old kitchens. In many of the remodeling jobs she had done, she had often had the opportunity to decorate living rooms and bedrooms in authentic period styles. When it came to kitchens, though, the word was always, "I want my kitchen modern. You know, formica, linoleum, dropped ceiling with fluorescent lighting, and figure in a microwave oven, won't you?"

It was the customer's house. What else could she do? But Hamilton had given no such orders.

Stacy peered into the old kitchen; she could see the bare branches of the lilac bush outside pressed against the window. She sighed. "Oh, Tom. Look at the size."

"The cabinets are rotted."

"All right. We'll find others. But they've got to be right, with wood counters, and the floor has got to be natural, and this room could hold an old wood stove in that corner with a round oak table in front of it."

In her mind's eye, she could see the gray dust-filled gloom and the ancient linoleum replaced by shining wooden surfaces, high-backed chairs, bright woven carpets, modern appliances hidden in the alcove, and a cheery wood stove to warm a winter evening.

Tom's eyes narrowed and he peered into her face. "You sound like a woman planning her own home when you talk about the kitchen and nursery, Stacy."

"Look," she said, catching his arm and guiding him to the kitchen window. "It's perfect. There should be a gravel path from the back door, and to the left I'd have the kitchen garden, and to the right the cutting garden. Then outside that other window, where you can see it from the table, I'd put in a perennial bed with a background hedge of laurentinas, so that it wouldn't be bare in winter."

"How much money did you get?" Tom asked.

Stacy shrugged. "About enough for the front entry hall and ten feet into the parlor. Never mind. That ten feet is going to knock Mr. Hamilton right between the eyes, and I'll get the whole job. I have to!"

She swung toward Tom and her eyes shone. "I have to do this place! Not just for the money. I really love this house!"

Tom nodded. They had known each other since first grade and, although he was as friendly as a neighbor's dog, he was usually completely impersonal with her. Sometimes, though, he surprised her with his insights.

"Of course," he said. "I knew you would. I've been in here before, and when Laura told me you were coming here, I knew what would happen."

Stacy's eyes widened. "What do you mean?"

"This place is a lot like your parents' old house."

Stacy felt a stab of pain. She had blocked her old home from her mind. It was on the north edge of the Island and hidden from the road by a long, winding drive. That meant she never had to see it, and she intentionally did not go to look at it. She knew that it would only be a cold, empty reminder of happier times.

"It—it's not the same. Not at all."

"Yes, it is," Tom said quietly. "It only looks different from the outside. Change the roof and add a porch halfway around—"

"It—yes, I suppose—oh, Tom, I wish you hadn't said it."

"I thought you knew. I'm sorry."

"No, it's only—I'm not sure I can do it now."

"Stacy, I thought you already found out you couldn't run away from the past."

"I thought so, too." She walked into the front hall, stared up at the fan window, remembered a diamond window set above another doorway, turned, pictured her mother's carpet on the stairs, blinked, and shook her head. "You're right, of course. It is very similar. I think it's the atmosphere rather than the actual structure. But it isn't their home. Birch House is itself and I won't decorate it to match my memories. It has its own personality."

Tom's arm slipped comfortably around her shoulder. "Come on, we'll beat the rain back to town."

He was a minute too late. As he dashed to his truck and Stacy ran to her car, a scattering of raindrops blew into her face and ruffled her short black hair.

Chapter Two

For the next few days, Stacy barely saw the inside of the office, which was the way she liked to work. Paperwork was the boring side of the business.

She conferred with Phillips on the remodeling and picked everything from roofing materials to plumbing fixtures for him. Then she spent two days scouting out old cabinet doors for Tom to refinish and install over the new kitchen cabinets Phillips would build. On one trip she found a fantastic light fixture with three art glass shades, which would set the character of the entry hall. But it wasn't until late the following afternoon that she found time to drive out to Birch House with the fixture to see it in the hall. If it did not suit the proportions, she could return it to the dealer.

When she parked on the road across from the house, she saw a truck and a car in the driveway. One of Phillips' men, perched on the steep roof of the house, was ripping away at the old shingles.

He shouted something and Stacy waved hello. She carried the metal ceiling fixture in her other hand. The glass shades remained in her car, packed carefully in a carton.

Inside, the house had not been touched. Stacy kicked aside the plaster chips that had been jarred loose by the pounding on the roof. When she wandered into the kitchen, she could not find the stepladder Phillips had promised to leave there for her. This did not especially surprise her, though; she had worked with Phillips before on small projects. He was pleasant but forgetful.

Stacy left the light fixture on the stove and walked to the back door. The handle turned easily enough, but the door would not open. She pulled with all her weight, then braced herself with one foot on the door frame and tugged again. Nothing. Disgusted, she hurried back through the house, out the front door, and up the drive to the old barn that served as a garage. She must remember to tell Phillips to get that door open.

A search through cobwebs and dust uncovered an old stepladder. Stacy hesitated, glanced down at her clean sweater and skirt, considered the long drive home to change clothes, sighed, and shouldered the ladder. It was heavy, but for a woman, Stacy was strong. By the time she had struggled down the drive and up to the front door, though, she was beginning to wonder if she had overestimated her strength. She set the ladder on the steps and reached for the doorknob. To her surprise, the door opened before she could touch it.

"Miss Green! I thought I heard someone." Mr. Hamilton stared at her, and from the stiff expression on his handsome face, Stacy knew all too well how she looked. She was perspiring, and she guessed correctly that her damp forehead and short dark hair wore a veil of dust and cobwebs. She started to brush them away, looked at her hands, saw how filthy they were from handling the old ladder, and shrugged.

"Good afternoon, Mr. Hamilton." She usually said "hi," but this time she felt the need to balance her appearance with a more elegant greeting.

"Isn't that ladder too heavy for you?"

"Yes," she said, and added maliciously, "would you lift it inside for me?"

He didn't hesitate or even glance down at his beautiful suit. Before his hands touched the ladder, Stacy said, "No, don't," and pushed his arm aside. Her conscience had a bad habit of striking her at odd times. "It's so dirty," she explained. "I can manage it."

She lifted the ladder and pushed past him into the entry. He watched silently as she set it up. Then she disappeared into the kitchen and returned to the hall a moment later with the fixture in her grubby hand. She climbed up the ladder until, reaching above her head, she could hold the fixture approximately in place.

"How's that?" she asked.

"Fine."

"Fine?" Stacy sat down on the top of the stepladder and stared at him. He took the fixture from her outstretched hands and put it in the corner. "That fixture holds three genuine Quezal art glass shades, and it is going to cost you eight hundred dollars. If you only think it is 'fine,' I can buy you a replica fixture for a third of the cost."

"I like that one, Miss Green."

"Do you really?" she demanded. She wanted so much for him to show some of the enthusiasm she felt for the house.

Instead, he said flatly, "Actually, I don't have any opinion one way or the other. I'll take your word that the fixture is correct for the house. That's what I am paying you for."

"Maybe you'd like it better if I showed you the shades. They're the beautiful part," Stacy said hopefully. "I thought I would pick up the colors in the shades for the wallpaper."

He gazed at her thoughtfully but didn't answer.

Silence always drove Stacy to talk too much and too rapidly. She rushed on, "Since there isn't a hall closet, I'm looking for an oak wardrobe. The right one, against that wall, would make the entry perfect, don't you think, especially when the stairs and balustrade are refinished and set off by a light paper. Tom says the floors are cedar, so we'll play up their color, and then if you want to go the price, a small Oriental rug that would leave the edges of the floor exposed. That would be elegant with the Quezal shades, but of course, it isn't necessary or it could be added later. To really suit, it should be an old rug worn soft, or else something local in a handwoven or a braid. I found some cabinet doors that Tom will refinish and they are authentic Northwest because . . ."

"Miss Green," he interrupted, "do whatever you want."

"Don't you care?" Stacy asked.

"I care that it looks right."

"But that's the trouble. I don't know your idea of right. I can do the whole thing in antiques of any period as long as they are older than the house, and in practically any price range—"

"What period would be most suitable?"

Did he look bored? Stacy ignored that thought. She tried to waken his interest with her own enthusiasm. "I've dug several old photo albums out of friends' attics and studied the interiors of these houses when they were new, and honestly, if I were doing it for myself, I'd try to duplicate the old cottage furniture, but I'd want to brighten the effect with lighter walls, enlargement of some window areas, bright upholstery—"

"That sounds fine."

"Then you aren't using the house as a backdrop for rare antiques? So many people do."

"No."

"Oh, I am glad. If you have any family pieces, I would like to see them so that we could work them into the design—"

"No, nothing."

"So I will definitely work toward early cottage, and what I would really like to do is include the garden, you know, replant it as it must have been. But maybe you don't want to go into landscaping?"

He nodded. "Do that, too." Then he pulled a car key from his pocket and turned toward the door.

"You're not leaving?" Stacy cried, and started down the ladder. Her foot missed a step; she slipped, yelped, grabbed for air, and then clung wildly to the strong shoulders of Mr. Hamilton as he whirled around and grabbed her.

He set her firmly on her feet.

"Oh, I am so sorry!" Stacy cried, as her hands slid off his shoulders, leaving dust tracks on the light gray wool.

He glanced at his suit. "You are something of a menace, Miss Green," he said.

"Oh! Oh, let me take your coat down to the cleaners. Jack will fix that up for you while you wait."

"You seem to know everyone on the Island."

"I grew up here. I am terribly sorry about your coat."

"Then why did you soar out at me like Wonder Woman?"

"I didn't mean to!" Stacy sputtered. "I caught my foot on the ladder, and anyway, I only wanted you to stay a few more minutes, because there really are some points you should consider, and then there are things I need to know. But never mind, right now we should get that coat fixed—"

"Forget the coat," he said firmly. "I think the best thing to do would be to go over your questions and get them answered before you leap at me again from a ladder. Then I will go off by myself in my own car and take care of my own coat problem."

Stacy's small mouth turned down in a comical frown; it was an odd contrast to her straight, elegant nose, and for a moment, she thought he might laugh. But if humor had flickered in his gray eyes, he had managed to control it.

"What is your first question?"

"All right, we'll start with the parlor." She led him into it and pointed to the small window. "I would like to replace that with glass-paned double doors that would open onto a patio. A gravel patio would be perfect with perhaps an octagonal bench built around the cherry tree, but maybe you prefer brick? Do you?"

"Answer to question one. Put in the doors and any kind of patio you like."

"All right. Not as much help as I had hoped for, but on to the next question. Do you have any opinions about the kitchen? Would you like a wood stove near the table?"

"My answer to that, and this is my final answer on this subject, is that I don't have any opinions about kitchens. My cook will work in anything that contains all the modern appliances, so put them in, but figure out how to make it look traditional. That cover that?"

"Yes, but it brings up my next question. How many people are going to live in this house?"

"Live in it? We'll be using it for occasional weekends, that's all."

"For occasional weekends?" Stacy squeaked. She stopped, forcing herself to lower her voice, and added, "But what about the gardens? Perhaps I'd better put it all in shrubs, or we could fill in with native plants, you know, ferns, rhododendron, salal—they wouldn't require maintenance."

"I want regular gardens and we'll hire someone to maintain them. Maybe I'll have a housekeeper living here, I don't know."

"There's a small servants' wing off the kitchen," Stacy said. "At least, it could be. Probably it was extra bedrooms, which I was thinking of turning into a library. But perhaps you'd rather have it redone as it is—two bedrooms and a bath."

"That would be fine."

"But what if I had gone ahead and had Phillips convert it into a library or something else?" Stacy asked.

"If we want anything changed later, we'll change it."

"That's an awful waste of money!"

"You aren't hired to handle my finances," he said. "Just decorate my house. Now, are there any more questions?"

"Just one. When you are here on weekends, how many of you will there be? I have to know so that I can plan the bedroom arrangements. I rather thought I would convert the small bedroom into a bath-dressing room to adjoin the master bedroom."

"Fine. There will only be the servants and myself and, of course, my wife."

Why had she assumed he was single? Because on all her other jobs she had worked mainly with the wife, and so when this man came alone to order a job, she assumed he had no wife.

Stacy kept a calm face with effort and asked, "Wouldn't Mrs. Hamilton like to go over the plans with me? Surely she must have color preferences."

"Miss Green, you now know everything you need to know to decorate this place. The only requirements are that it be functional, authentically decorated, and let's see, I believe the other two explicit directions were for 'uniqueness' and 'charm.' "

"Then Mrs. Hamilton isn't interested in the house?" Stacy blurted. As soon as she had said it, she realized how rude it sounded. She stared at him, wide eyed, wondering if she should apologize.

He gazed down at her, the expression in his light eyes unfathomable, his slender, strong face a quiet mask. To her surprise, he reached out and brushed her forehead with his fingers.

"Cobwebs don't become you," he said softly.

"I gather lots of them in this job."

"You must ruin lots of clothes."

"I hadn't planned to dig through the old barn today," Stacy said. "Next time I come out I'll be in my coveralls. You should, too."

For the first time since she had met him, he smiled. His even teeth shone white in his tanned face. "I don't think I own any."

"If you're going to remodel an old house, you should buy some," she said.

"I am not going to remodel an old house. You are. But I hope you leave the lifting and hauling to Phillips. You were hired to do the planning."

"You'd be surprised how much lifting and hauling there can be to planning. It isn't a neat desk job, Mr. Hamilton. I spent the last three days crawling around old barns and auction houses and antique shop storerooms, trying to find the right cabinet doors for the kitchen. But it was worth it. Wait until you see them. Actually, I would rather you didn't see them until Tom has refinished them. They don't look like anything now but they are going to be fantastic. And when we open up that side window in the kitchen, you'll have a view across the perennial border. Did I tell you I'm planning a perennial border, right to the hedge? You'll love it—"

He cut in. "I am sure it will be fine. I have to get back to town."

Stacy rubbed her hands together to wipe away some of the dust.

"All right," she said. "I'm glad I ran into you today. With the information you've given me, we can get underway. Is there any sort of time schedule, Mr. Hamilton? Phillips works better under a time schedule. Mind you, he won't be finished when he says he will, but at least if you pin him down to a date he should be done within the following month."

"And what about you?"

"Oh, I stick right to time schedules. If I tell you a job will be done, it will be, but then I can't go any faster than the contractors, you understand. However, I can push them and do a lot of phoning and shouting."

He raised his eyebrows and looked doubtful. "Do they listen to you?"

Stacy planted her fists firmly on her slim hips and raised her pointed chin at a defiant angle. Her dark eyes sparkled. "I am a very good nagger, and although Phillips and Tom may not live in trembling fear of me, they do hustle to shut me up."

"You do talk a lot," he said.

"Well, I never!"

He grinned. "Do you need that ladder carried around to the barn?"

"Not by you, Mr. Fancy Pants," Stacy retorted.

His face went blank but she thought he was fighting back laughter. The man had far too much control. He walked calmly out of the house without so much as a good-bye, and it wasn't until he reached his car that Stacy, watching him from the doorway, thought to ask her last question.

"Mr. Hamilton! Wait. I meant to ask. Shall I make that front room with the bay window into a nursery?"

He stared at her for a moment without answering. Then he said slowly, "I think I should get married first."

Stacy stood openmouthed as he backed his car out of the driveway and disappeared around the bend of Sunday Road.

Had she heard him correctly? First he had talked about the master bedroom being for himself and his wife, then he had said he should get married.

Back to one down and two across on this puzzle, Stacy decided. Not that his marital arrangements were any of her concern. She knew they weren't. So why did she wonder about his wife, and whether or not he had children? Ridiculous. He had hired her to decorate his weekend house, not to pry into his private life. But that was part of decorating, wasn't it? Not prying, of course, but matching a house to the family and living style. Most people told her far more about themselves than she wanted to know, sometimes revealing private details of their lives when she asked if they had hobbies that would require special areas in the house.

Stacy left the ladder in the house for future use and returned to her office. When she walked in, Laura looked up and said, "You practicing for Halloween?"

"It's already March. I don't like to be caught unprepared," Stacy said, stopping in front of the narrow mirror on the wall to comb the rest of the dust and cobwebs from her hair. She rubbed her face and hands with a tissue. "Someday, when we make it big, we are going to have an office with a washroom," she added.

"Terrific. In the meantime I'll be happy if we can pay the phone bill. How is the Hamilton job going?"

"I think we're in the open on that," Stacy said. She sat down at her desk and reached for the phone. "He was out at Birch House today and I guess he liked my plans. At least, he okayed them so we have the whole job."

"Terrific!"

"I'll have to complete some estimates but—" she listened to the phone ring at the other end, then said into the receiver, "Hello, John? Stacy Green. Couple of questions on the Birch House . . . yes, it's going well. Listen, I'm trying to plan living areas and Mr. Hamilton is very vague. Have you talked to Mrs. Hamilton . . . there isn't? I see . . . oh, in June. Of course, that explains a few things, but I wonder why she hasn't come in to talk to me . . . oh. Yes, I think so. Well, thanks."

"I love listening to half of conversations," Laura said. "Let me guess the answers. Hamilton bought Birch House to hide away his mad wife, like Mr. Rochester in *Jane Eyre,* since she is due to be released from the insane asylum in June, along with her father who thinks he is Dracula. And poor Mr. Hamilton, despite all his wealth, cannot find another asylum who will accept this weird pair and so . . ."

"You should be writing TV plots instead of decorating boudoirs. Speaking of boudoirs, how is the job for Webster coming along?"

"My dear, Mrs. Webster loves it and Mr. Webster hates it and I am caught in the middle, but we're going to solve all that with an easy chair in the corner, which was what Mr. Webster wanted in the first place." Laura's upturned nose wrinkled in her round face. "Sometimes I feel more like a marriage counselor than a decorator."

"I promised you variety in this job," Stacy teased.

"Yes, now tell me about Mr. Hamilton's mad wife."

"Oh, that. He is not married now, according to John, but he will be married in June to an exotic lady with an exotic name—that's John's description, not mine. The house is some casual little thing that she thought might be amusing, so he is buying it for her as a wedding present. Plus a honeymoon in Europe and probably more, but John didn't go into that. He just grabbed the money and signed the papers."

"How romantic."

"Do you really think so?"

"I can't think of anything more romantic than a man who buys a house that will cost a fortune to remodel and then classifies it as a casual little gift."

"Maybe you should marry a rich man, too," Stacy teased.

Then she phoned Tom to check his progress on refinishing the doors, and returned the dentist's call to reassure him that she was almost done with his office plans.

"I could take over that job," Laura said, "if you're going to be tied up with the Birch House."

"Now that I've started, I'll go over the plans with him, but then I'll let you track down the fabrics," Stacy said. "There isn't any hurry on the Birch House. John said this European honeymoon will last all summer, so we probably have until September to finish it."

"How strange. Still, I suppose they want to be sure it's done when they return."

"John got the impression that they really didn't care."

"Then why did they buy it?"

"I don't know," Stacy said. "I wish I did. It is truly odd. John said that Mr. Hamilton and his future wife came in looking for a house typical of the early development period of the Island, something run down that needed a complete remodel. John was delighted to unload Birch House because it was in need of so much work that he knew it would be practically impossible to find a buyer who could handle it. Of course, since money is nothing to Hamilton, he snapped it up. Then before he came to see me, he did an odd thing."

"Ordered bars for the upstairs windows for his father-in-law?"

"Will you stop that? No, listen, he hired a professional photographer to come out and do a complete set of photos of the place."

"What for?"

"John hasn't a clue. He did say that the bride is busy with her wedding plans, which is why I probably haven't seen her, and that he expects she'll breeze in one day. She's the breeze-in type, he says."

"I can hardly wait," Laura said. "But in the meantime, since we are not brides-to-be of wealthy men, or of anyone for that matter, I guess we better act like working girls and straighten out that last bank statement."

"We could do that," Stacy agreed, "or we could call it quits for the day, lock up, and head home."

"Do you know, I'd like that."

Stacy had known, which was why she made the suggestion. With all the strange conversations of the day whirling in her mind, she knew she could not concentrate on the bank statement. If she tackled it when her mind was fresh, first thing in the morning, it would be simple enough.

One great asset in working with Laura was that whenever Stacy mentioned ending the day and going home, Laura's mind immediately swung to thoughts of dinner.

Food was Laura's strongest interest. She pushed back
her chair and moved around the desk to reach her
coat, her plump body wedged between the desk and the
wall hook. She made an interesting contrast to Stacy.
Laura was plump, fair haired, round faced and blue
eyed, almost the reverse of Stacy, even to the slow,
motherly smile in contrast with Stacy's grin.

As they drove up to their building, Laura said, "Why
don't you take a long soak in the tub while I fix the
hamburgers?"

Stacy laughed. "Are you trying to say you don't want
to eat across the table from my dirty hands?"

"Oh, no, I didn't mean that."

"Of course you did. Grab the paper, will you?"

While Stacy unlocked their apartment door, Laura
collected the mail and the paper from the hall table.
They had all their business and personal mail delivered
to their office, but the postman still left junk mail for
their apartment.

"There's an ad from the drugstore, the cut-rate store
and, oh, let's see, oh, some sort of gigantic giveaway
contest from a magazine subscription company."

"Terrific." Stacy dropped her purse on the table inside the door and hung her sweater in the closet. "I
think I'll take you up on that hot bath offer if you don't
mind fixing supper tonight."

"Ummm. Go ahead." Laura wandered into the
kitchen with the paper in her hand. "Here Priscilla,
here puss."

"If you're going to make our supper, I can surely
take care of Priscilla," Stacy offered, taking the cat
food can and opener from the shelf. "Here puss, puss."

They heard the bedsprings twang softly, followed by
Priscilla's flat-footed landing on the floor. By the time
Stacy had filled Priscilla's dish, the cat's white face
was peering around the corner of the kitchen doorway.

"If you were a dog, you would greet us at the door
when we came home and not wait until I fixed your
supper," Stacy scolded.

Priscilla ambled slowly across the floor and rubbed

against Stacy's legs. Stacy scratched the white ears and ran her fingers over the long white fur of the Persian. "You get fatter and lazier every day, puss."

Laura flipped the pages of the newspaper that she had spread out on the kitchen counter. As Stacy started to head toward the bathroom, Laura exclaimed, "Look here!"

"What is it?"

"Your exotic mystery lady with the exotic name!"

Stacy bent over the paper and peered at the picture. It was a typical newspaper picture, gray and rather poorly printed, but it obviously represented one of those very expensive studio portraits done in a popular casual pose. The woman was very blond, very glamorous, and beneath the picture the caption named her as one Dominic Rouse, and announced her planned wedding date in June to Avery Hamilton.

"At least we know what she looks like," Laura said.

"Ummm. About what I expected."

"Really? She doesn't look to me like a collector of old houses."

"Maybe not, but she looks like what Avery Hamilton would collect. She'll go well with his custom-made suits."

Laura gave Stacy a quizzical look. "That doesn't sound like you, Stace."

Stacy shrugged. "Guess I'm tired. Mr. Hamilton is a difficult man to work with, and my nerves are a bit raw."

She left Priscilla picking fussily at the cat food and Laura collecting things for supper. Closing the door on the rattle of pans, Stacy ran a hot bath, stripped, and slowly sank into the water. It relaxed her body but not her mind. Dominic Rouse. Yes, it was an exotic name. She looked like a woman who belonged in a penthouse or a city mansion staffed with servants, not in an old, renovated country cottage. When Birch House was completed, would the two of them wander through the evening dusk along the gravel paths, arms linked, dressed in their expensive suits?

Stacy visualized those two perfect profiles turned at

elegant angles to survey the distant water view. For them a full moon would rise and send a silver path across the sea to their feet. Why did she see them as an Art Deco painting? It was the elegance, she guessed, the rigid perfection of their handsome faces, his crowned with dark red hair, hers framed in gold. Or was she a silver-blond? In an Art Deco picture she would be a silver-blond, but perhaps in real life her hair was light brown and her nose was covered with freckles.

"Not that it matters," Stacy told the soap. "Whatever they look like, they have thrown a very nice job my way and heaven knows, we needed it. A client who will pay on time—now that is a decorator's dream."

She closed her eyes, relaxed in the warmth of the water, and remembered, without meaning to, the way his hands had circled her waist when he lifted her down from the ladder.

"It is nice to have a wealthy client," Stacy muttered to herself, "but he would be a lot easier to work with if he were about fifty percent homelier."

Chapter Three

Stacy did not have to wait long to find out the exact shade of Dominic Rouse's hair.

Spring sunlight poured through the plate-glass window fronting the office, lighting the interior and creating a pool of warmth on the extra chair. Priscilla, who had decided to come to work today, curled her chin around on her paws and rested from the exertion of the ride to the office. Occasionally, she opened one sleepy eye to cast a glance of disapproval at the ringing phone. When the office door opened, she pulled her fluffy tail around her like a quilt to cut out the draft.

Sunlight glowed on the halo of pale blond hair. Stacy glanced up, saw the face that had posed so elegantly in her imaginary Art Deco illustration, and carefully said, "Good morning."

She had almost added "Miss Rouse," but had caught herself in time. Stacy did not want her client to think that she was the center of gossip or spying, and a lengthy explanation about seeing her marriage announcement picture in the paper would be a strain. At the moment Stacy wasn't quite sure why it would be a strain, she only knew instinctively that it would be.

"Good morning. Are you Miss Green?" With a somewhat disconcerting glance, Dominic Rouse looked at both Stacy and Laura.

Laura said no and Stacy said yes.

"I see. I am Miss Rouse. I believe you are in charge of the remodeling project on my house."

"Yes, Birch House."

"Birch House?"

"That's what it's called," Stacy explained. "Has been

for years. Because of the birches. In the front yard. You know."

"Are there? I suppose I didn't notice."

Dominic Rouse made Stacy feel like a stupid child staring up at a rather overbearing schoolteacher. Pushing back her chair, she said, "Would—uh—would you like to go out to the house? I mean, I suppose you would like to go over it with me and tell me in some detail what you want done to it."

Dominic sniffed, or at least it sounded like a sniff to Stacy, but the perfect face with its chiseled features and careful make-up showed no emotion.

"I hadn't planned on that. I presume you know what you're doing."

Stacy gazed wide eyed and tried to look competent and intelligent. For all her usual glibness, she could not think of a thing to say in reply.

"Actually I came in to make quite certain that you understood what is expected. Avery can be a bit vague, I know, and, although he assured me he gave you explicit instructions, I did want to confirm the information."

Explicit instructions. Stacy cleared her throat to cover her hesitation as she remembered him telling her to do whatever she wanted and to use her own favorite color. "Well, uh, I did talk to Mr. Hamilton, of course, but he was—well, you know how men are. That is, I would like to discuss this with you further." She plucked Priscilla from the chair, plopped her down on the window ledge, and gestured to Miss Rouse. "Do sit down. I would like to go over colors with you and any special effects you want."

"Colors? I hadn't thought—quite a lot of white, I should suppose, or perhaps not."

"Certainly we'll use light backgrounds. Old houses tend to be dark, otherwise, especially with the natural wood tones in the woodwork and floors."

"I understood you had done redecorations on several older homes and were an expert in the field."

"Oh. That's very kind."

"I didn't mean it as flattery. Avery's lawyer had you

investigated, and he said you had done rooms in a house that was on a home tour that received very good publicity."

Stacy's mind whirled. Investigated! Fascinating. When she had been with the Seattle firm, she had done three rooms in a house that was later widely photographed. It was indeed her one claim to real publicity, but since opening the Island office a year ago, she had almost forgotten about it. The Islanders weren't interested in artistic design, they simply wanted practical, easy-care decoration.

"I see," she said. "Did you see the photographs of that house? It wasn't like Birch House, it was a Victorian Gothic."

"The point is, the lawyer said you knew how to do authentic period remodeling and that you could make it very attractive and original. That is what I want."

"I'm glad you came in," Stacy said truthfully. "I've been trying to pin Mr. Hamilton down to a few more facts, and I'm sure you and I can pinpoint exactly what you want. There are several ways we can go with Birch House. We can almost do without structural changes, keep the furniture very low-key cabin, and make you a comfortable hideaway, or we can simply stick with the period and dress it up with somewhat better-quality pieces, aiming at making it a suitable year-round residence."

"Residence? No, that doesn't matter." Dominic frowned ever so slightly, as though she were aware of what a deep frown would do to her complexion. She leaned forward and said earnestly, "I have a friend who bought an old house in Maine and she had it completely redone. *Homes of Distinction* sent out photographers and did a complete layout on the house. In fact, several of my friends in the East have had their homes or summer homes done, but as far as I know none of them have ever had a place on an island way out here in Puget Sound. I mean, most of them don't know what Puget Sound is! It would really be exciting, don't you think, to have that house we bought covered by a national magazine?"

"You bought the house so that it could be remodeled and featured in *Homes of Distinction?*"

"I thought it would be an exciting project. And of course your name would be mentioned as the interior designer, Miss Green."

"Well, but surely, that is, I mean, you must have some idea about using the house. You do want to live there sometimes, don't you?"

"Oh, yes. Sometime. That is, we aren't on the West Coast very often, you know, but Avery does make trips here several times a year, and I am told that the Island is very charming in the summer."

Stacy nodded. She did not dare look at Laura. Suddenly the whole quick cash sale of Birch House to the unlikely Mr. Hamilton fell into place. Birch House was a trinket, a toy, a little hobby to amuse a spoiled fiancée who probably moved in very jet-set type circles and liked to see herself featured in society columns and slick, fashionable magazines. She knew that Laura would have her head bent over paperwork on her desk, but her ears and mind would be concentrated on this whole conversation. If they looked at each other, they would either have to laugh or cry. It was funny, it really was, but it was pathetic too, because for both of them the Island was the promised land, and its old houses were a part of the history and friendship of its inhabitants. They were not toys.

"I understand," Stacy said slowly, knowing that Miss Dominic Rouse would be amazed if she knew the full truth of that statement. "We will make Birch House historically correct, but at the same time, the emphasis will be on charm and uniqueness. Come to think of it, that is exactly what Mr. Hamilton told me he wanted, even though I didn't quite appreciate his full meaning."

"Oh, and something else," Miss Rouse said. "You know how those articles always mention how something—maybe baskets on the kitchen wall or clocks in the master bedroom—is part of a collection of the owner? If you could think of something of that sort—and also, I do think there should be some treasures."

While Stacy's mind digested the idea of creating a

collection for a noncollector, it balked at the word "treasures." She asked, "Say that again?"

"Treasures. An occasional piece that can be mentioned or used as a focus. A rare, really rare antique or something like that. Something almost, oh, museum quality, or perhaps something tied in with local history. Do you know what I mean?"

"I—" Stacy paused, thought seriously of telling Miss Rouse that homeowners created their own collections through years of love and interest. Then she considered the state of the office finances, and said, "I think so. I'm sure I can find some interesting pieces for you."

"I am sure you can," Miss Rouse said and gave Stacy a rather angelic smile. She would certainly make a gorgeous bride with that beautiful face and full figure. For some odd reason Stacy caught herself fervently hoping that Miss Rouse was as sweet as her smile and not as shallow as the "little project" that seemed to have been planned mostly to impress her friends.

"I did find a very interesting light fixture for the entry hall," Stacy said, "and I wondered if it would be too much, but now that I understand what you want, I think it is perfect. It is the sort of thing *Homes of Distinction* likes to feature because it is authentic and a collector's item. I was worried about the price; however, Mr. Hamilton seemed to think the price was no problem. With most projects, the owners prefer to okay any purchases of that sort, but of course the dealer would allow me to return it, so I went ahead and took the chance—" Stacy listened to her own voice rattling on and wished she could shut up, but whenever she was nervous she talked more than she wanted to.

Miss Rouse said, "Don't worry about prices. Mr. Hamilton will be agreeable as long as the result is satisfactory. I do think we understand each other, Miss Green, and I do think it is a sweet touch to have a real Islander doing the decorating. You'll excuse me now because I really must take the next ferry back. Avery is waiting for me at the realtor's office."

"Oh, he's on the Island?"

"Yes, a matter of some papers to be picked up or

something, and he suggested I drop by to see you. It's been very pleasant. Good afternoon." As Miss Rouse moved gracefully out of the door, Stacy bit back a gasp. Miss Dominic Rouse's elegantly clad derrière was covered with white cat fur.

After the door closed, Laura said, "I have thought of calling you many things, my dear, but never a *sweet touch.*"

Stacy rolled her wide black eyes. "Imagine. A real live Islander to be the decorator. I hope she doesn't want me photographed in beads and a skirt of salal leaves."

"Just think of yourself as a part of her collection."

"Surely she didn't really mean it that way? Probably she is a very nice person and we don't know her well enough."

"I am more than willing to give the benefit of the doubt to anyone who can make this firm solvent," Laura said.

"It isn't just the money. I want her to be nice."

"Why?"

Laura's blunt question snapped Stacy back to reality. In her mind's eye she had been visualizing Avery Hamilton's face, and how his eyes had been strangely soft in that one quick moment when his fingers brushed her face. He might be harsh and impatient on the outside, but she knew that behind the act was a man who deserved to be loved.

Fiddlesticks. He was a client. Why was she standing around daydreaming like a teenager? Annoyed with her own thoughts, Stacy buried herself in paperwork to make the morning pass more quickly. It was her least favorite task, and when Laura went out to a job and she remained behind, she felt as though she were punishing herself. For what? For having such dumb thoughts, she told herself firmly, and then found herself daydreaming again.

If he were on the Island, why hadn't he stopped by the office with Miss Rouse?

When Tom phoned and asked her to meet him at Birch House, she jumped at the excuse to hang the

"Be Back Soon" sign in the window. Grabbing Priscilla, Stacy locked up the office and hurried to her car.

"Come on, puss, you can go for a drive with me. There's a nice tangled hillside for you to explore."

Priscilla purred her agreement. She always enjoyed car rides.

At Birch House Stacy carried Priscilla to the front step, set her down, and let her go. Priscilla streaked through the tangle of weeds to the hedge and disappeared.

Tom was in the kitchen, holding a refinished cabinet door up against the wall. "What do you think in this light?"

"Yes, I think so."

"Too much red? I can tone it down with a duller oil."

"No, I kind of like that. It should go well with the floors."

"All right. Now if we can wander through here and you can tell me the colors and finishes you want, I can order paints and stains while Phillips finishes his ripping out. As soon as he's through banging on the roof, I'll start on the back bedroom. I don't suppose this could be a pay-as-you-go job?"

"You bet it can! Turn in your hours to me every Friday and I'll hit you with a check and Mr. Hamilton with a bill."

"Sewed up that tight?"

Stacy nodded. All she had to do was keep *Homes of Distinction* magazine's criteria in the back of her mind, and she could keep this job to the last driveway pebble. It was the best, biggest, and perhaps most creative opportunity she had ever been given. Why then did she feel depressed? As they wandered through the rooms, she thought she knew. Her imagination filled each room with laughter and children and family activities, because that was what Birch House was meant for. Consciously, though, she knew that it would stand empty most of the time, and that the only sounds would be the clicking of *Homes of Distinction* cameras.

"Hope I didn't pull you away from something really important," Tom said.

"No. I'm weary of hearing that phone ring. It is odd, isn't it, that I'm so busy all the time and yet I'm barely paying the bills? I always thought that if we reached a point where we had a constant flow of jobs, we'd be rich."

Tom laughed. "Stacy, I wish your reasoning were true. I work a good sixty-hour week and I still can't afford to get married."

"Maybe this job will help."

"Oh, I'm going to get married, anyway, afford it or not. Angie and I are both sick of waiting."

"Good for you," Stacy said firmly and meant it. She liked Angie.

"What about you?" Tom asked. "You can't stay single forever."

Stacy grinned at him. "I'll have to, won't I, now that you are marrying Angie?"

Tom's eyes twinkled. He said solemnly, "If only I had met you before first grade it would be a different story. But I was already promised to Angie by then. She told me in kindergarten that we were going to marry."

"She probably did, at that," Stacy said. Angie and Tom had lived next door to each other since infancy. "At least no one can say you're marrying in haste."

"As long as I'm spoken for, there must be someone else you could care for," Tom said.

"Uh-uh. You'd think so. Only every time I meet a guy I could really care about, he finds me boring. And vice versa."

"Maybe you're too devoted to your career to be a wife."

"I don't think so. I think if I met the right man, everything else would fall in place."

"Isn't that the truth?" Tom agreed. "Have you picked the paper for this room?"

"No, but I will tomorrow. Why don't you write down how many double rolls we'll need for each room so that I can get the orders in?"

"Right. Sometimes it takes weeks to get the paper."

"No hurry," Stacy said. "They don't want the place until next September so we have all the time we want."

"What about this room?"

Stacy peered into the beautiful front bedroom, its dingy gray paper stained and torn, its bay window black with dust. She imagined the way it would be, bright with flowered paper and a handwoven rug and a bentwood rocker. She would find suitable beds for a guest room, but what it really needed was a child's bed, a crib, and in the far corner a toy cupboard and a rocking horse. She could even imagine a child, surrounded by picture books, curled up on a thick velvet cushion in the bay window.

Shaking her head to return herself to the present, she said, "Go ahead on the woodwork and floors whenever you want. No structural changes here."

"Then I guess that does it," Tom said as they turned to go downstairs.

In the front entry hall Tom sat on a step and figured out from the room dimensions how much paper he would need. Meanwhile, Stacy stood in the open doorway and gazed out across the long slope of Sunday Hill with its stands of fir, cleared meadows, and an old apple orchard of gnarled trees. She could see all the way to the lower row of beach houses clustered like a miniature town at the water's edge. Today the sea reflected the calm blue sky, bright and cloudless. It was one of the "lamb" days of March. Soon the meadows would bloom with wild flowers and the fir trees would sprout new, bright green tips on their dark branches. Between the sea and sky the Olympic mountains shone white in the sun.

"I think I would like a very wide gravel path at the base of these stairs. I think I'll have it wide enough to accommodate a couple of benches."

"Did I tell you we're getting married in June?" Tom asked.

Stacy turned in the doorway to face him. "Everyone is getting married in June."

"Everyone?"

"The people who are buying this house, anyway. I met her today, the woman who will own it. She is very anxious that the house be up to the standards of *Homes of Distinction* magazine."

"*Homes of Distinction* on little old Corver Island?"

"You think I'm joking? These people are very rich but they are more than that. They, oh, how can I say it, they seem to be some sort of socialites back East, and having one's summer home appear in *Homes of Distinction* is a kind of status symbol. At least, I think it must be because she didn't much care about whether or not I decorated the house to suit their living style. She was much more concerned that it be acceptable as a magazine layout."

Tom frowned. "That is very weird. Here I am trying to figure out how to afford a house that will keep out the rain and the wind and the tax man, and there are people in the world who can buy houses to use for magazine layouts. Very weird."

"She seemed to think it was extremely important," Stacy said.

With a shrug, Tom said, "I suppose it's an obsession, you know, like people who try to have the world's largest collection of matchbook covers, or people who spend all their time entering sweepstake contests."

"Ummm. I can't really say much about the obsessions of the rich, having known so few rich people. I suppose it's harmless enough. I only wish—that it weren't Birch House."

"Why?"

"Oh, I don't know. I suppose it's dumb. But, honestly, I would rather see someone like you and Angie move in here. You would really live here, really make it a home."

"Don't I wish I could afford it! It has a great view."

"I guess I'd better get back to the office and the phone. Here Priscilla, puss, puss, puss," Stacy called.

She saw the grass twitch suspiciously on the far side of the lawn, but Priscilla did not emerge. "Come on, Priscilla, come now, time to go."

"If you were Priscilla, would you trade this sunny hunting ground for your office chair?"

"I don't have to be Priscilla to answer that one. I would much prefer to sit here in the sun all day."

"I'll be around for another hour, Stacy. Go ahead if you want, and I'll drop Priscilla off when I come through town. If I know her, she'll be bored by then and come wandering into the house to see what I'm doing."

Stacy called a few more times, gave up, and returned to town without the cat. As she drove she remembered the white hairs on Dominic Rouse's dark silk suit, and smiled. When she reached the office, Laura was out and a note was propped on her desk asking her to phone the telephone company. Stacy gasped, opened her desk drawer, and dug through the pile of bills. Blast. She had forgotten to pay that bill. No, not actually forgotten. She had put it on the bottom of the pile until she could find the money, but then, after she had deposited Mr. Hamilton's check, she had cleared up all the past-due bills except for the telephone bill, which had slipped under some other papers. Stacy dialed the phone company, poured out a long tale of the misplaced bill, and promised to put the check in the afternoon mail. Then she hung up and started to write the check. The phone rang.

"Leitzel-Green Design."

"Miss Green? This is Dominic Rouse. I wanted to call you and I do hope I haven't interrupted you, but I picked up the new *Homes of Distinction* and I knew you would be interested. One of their main articles covers a beach house of a dear friend of mine in Virginia. You'll see that even though the house is new, it contains much of what I had in mind. That is, I don't want my house to be *anything* like hers, but quite a point is made of emphasizing collections and individual, unique pieces of furniture. So I did want to point it out to you so that you could look at it. That way I know that you will know what I am looking for. By the way, I do see that her house has a name, and I rather remember that you mentioned that *my* house had a name, didn't

you? So, if you could perhaps find out something about
how old the name of my house is, and who thought it
up or something like that, well, it *would* be interesting,
don't you think?"

What Stacy thought was that when she read the article she would find that the house in Virginia had a
name that had a history. What she said was, "Of course,
Miss Rouse, I will look into the history of the name
Birch House."

"Birch House. That's it. Thank you, and do look at
the article."

"I will."

"And do keep in mind finding a few unique pieces."

"I certainly will."

"And—and don't worry about the price. You have
a phone number for Mr. Hamilton's secretary, don't
you?"

"Yes."

"Good. Because I was afraid that you might find
something really marvelous and then worry about the
expense. If that should happen, well, call him and he'll
be able to give you an okay."

Now why hadn't Mr. Hamilton told her that? Stacy
sighed with relief after she had hung up the phone. The
idea of making up expensive collections had not pleased
her at all—the responsibility could be enormous—but
if she could verify the limits, that made the project
easier. Not easy, just easier.

Should she make up a collection of plants, wig stands,
copper warming pans, Indian relics (now that would be
truly interesting Northwest, but would it appeal to Miss
Rouse?), bone china, wood carvings, first editions?
Presumably, the collection should be something highly
photogenic. Honestly, this collection thing seemed to
be an obsession. That was Tom's word and he was quite
right. It was Miss Rouse's obsession. Didn't she know
that collections represented personal hobbies and inter-
ests? How could she think that people hired interior
decorators to make up their collections? It was an
absurd idea, an absurd obsession. For that matter the
whole project—buying a house not to live in but to

impress a magazine and a social circle—seemed an absurd obsession.

Dominic Rouse, with her expensive hairdo and magnificent clothes and cultured voice, might not know much of the world beyond her own circle. Stacy could understand that. But Mr. Hamilton traveled the world in his business and certainly dealt with all sorts of people. Couldn't he see how shallow this whole project was? Or was that why he was so vague and rather brusque in his explanations? Was that why he was evasive?

A man in his position must be accustomed to giving detailed replies to questions. Stacy cupped her chin in her hand and stared thoughtfully at the ceiling light fixture. He had not seemed bright, alert, and decisive at all, yet he had to be. But that must be it! He must consider the whole project rather peculiar, and so he left it to her to handle, hoping that he was wrong and that others had given her similar assignments. Did he doubt his fiancée's obsession? But was it just Dominic Rouse's obsession? Did Mr. Hamilton share it?

Stacy's elbow slipped on the loose papers, her head jerked forward; papers, books, and a cold cup of coffee, forgotten since early morning, flew off the far side of the desk. She shrieked.

Just then, Tom opened the door, jumped back, lost his grip on Priscilla, and took off down the street after her, shouting, "Here kitty, here kitty!"

Stacy dashed around the desk, swerving around the wide wet circle of spilled coffee on the carpet. She stopped at the door, saw Tom's disappearing back, threw up her hands, and raced after him.

"Priscilla!"

Even as she ran out she knew it was hopeless. There is no possible way to catch a frightened cat. Even if Tom could run as fast as Priscilla, he would lose her when he stooped to pick her up. And Priscilla could cut around corners and under low objects. Stacy ran after them anyway, not wanting to abandon Tom. She finally caught up with him at the corner, panting heavily. He stared glumly at the blackberry vines that tangled in a dark mass at the vacant lot between the last store and the crossroad.

"Never mind," Stacy said. "Priscilla knows her way back to the office."

"I am awfully sorry. Why did you scream at me?"

"I didn't. Not at you. I just knocked over a cup of coffee. See, I had just hung up from talking to the phone company because I put their bill under some other papers, and I didn't find it even when I finally had the money to pay it. So it really was an oversight and unintentional, but they didn't find that very interesting, and they skipped over my whole explanation. So I was just going to write a check, but when I hung up the phone——"

"Stacy," Tom said gently, "go back to your office and wait for your cat. See you later."

"Am I talking too much?" Stacy demanded.

"I would never say that. 'Bye now."

Stacy wandered back to her office, mopped up the coffee, wrote the check for the phone bill, cleared her desk, and finished the sketches for the dentist's office. Then she called out the office door for Priscilla half-a-dozen times. She finally gave up, plugged in the coffee-pot, pulled her brown bag lunch from her desk drawer, and unwrapped her sandwich.

Priscilla poked her nose around the door and meowed.

"I must have a very aromatic sandwich," Stacy said and broke off a bit for the cat.

The phone rang.

Around a mouthful of sandwich, Stacy said, "Leitzel-Green Design. Good morning."

"I think it is afternoon, Miss Green."

"Mr. Hamilton?" Stacy almost choked swallowing the sandwich.

"Are you all right?"

"Ugh. Yes. I'm just choking to death on my sandwich."

"All right. I was afraid you'd fallen off another ladder."

"No, I never do that at lunch time."

"Miss Green, did Dominic explain to you what she wants done with the house?"

"Yes, I have a much better picture now."

"Good. I felt sure she could clear up the matter. I called now to tell you that we will both be leaving for New York tonight, and it did occur to me that questions might arise while we're gone. If so, phone my secretary; he can probably answer any of your questions, or if he can't, he will contact me. I will be in and out of my New York office. Also, submit your expense sheets to him and he will authorize funds."

Stacy felt suddenly cold, as though she had received bad news. For someone who was not too pleased about the plans for Birch House, why was she so emotionally involved in the house and its new owners? This was business, strictly business, she made herself remember and asked, "Will you be back to Seattle soon?"

"In a week or two, I expect. Why?"

"It is just—I hope you'll come see the progress on the house when you can."

There was a short silence on the other end of the line. Then he said, "I'll be gone for at least three months this summer. I am counting on you to supervise the whole project."

"I know. But by then we'll be far enough along that I will be absolutely sure of what you want."

"I rather thought you knew yourself exactly what the house should look like."

"I do," Stacy exclaimed. "I have an exact picture of what I want done in my mind; I've planned all the rooms and the exterior and most of the furnishing details, although I can't be sure about all the pieces. Since we're using antiques, a certain number of final decisions will rest on what is available—you understand, don't you, Mr. Hamilton—but the thing is that I cannot be sure that my mental picture necessarily matches *your* mental picture. So I suppose that the whole problem is that, although I know Birch House very well, I don't really know you very well—" Stacy stopped suddenly, thought back over what she had blurted, and wished she could go back and reword the last sentence. Instead, she ended lamely, "At least, I don't know your tastes."

There was a pause. Finally he said, "Do you usually know your clients well?"

"It helps. I decorate to match people's personalities."

Did he laugh? She thought so, but she wasn't sure. He said, his voice low and even, "Decorate the house to match *your* personality, Miss Green. That should make it fascinating. I'll see you in a week or two." The receiver clicked on his end.

Chapter Four

Two weeks rushed by without benefit of the presence of Mr. Hamilton or Miss Rouse. Since the construction business was in a slight slump and Phillips had nothing else to do, he was able to complete the re-roofing and rip out half the interior walls to accommodate the plumbing and wiring renovation. The old cabinets were ripped out of the kitchen, and he had knocked holes in the parlor wall for the glass doors and then in the kitchen wall for the window enlargement. Mostly, the interior of Birch House was a jumble of plaster, old boards, nails, rags, tools, and some junk that even Phillips couldn't identify.

Whenever a house renovation reached this point, Stacy suffered from a temporary depression. It came on a bit like the flu, with headaches and dizzy spells, and she felt no more desire to face clients than she would care to face a boyfriend if she were breaking out in spots.

She had just returned from an inspection trip to Birch House when Mr. Hamilton walked into the office and, without even saying good morning, suggested that they go view the progress. Despite his unfortunate choice of words—for it was hard to think of a Phillips mess as progress—he was still the handsomest man Stacy had ever had walk into her office.

With an effort at keeping things on a businesslike basis, and avoiding a long hysterical explanation of Phillips' methods, Stacy said, "This is possibly not the best time to bother the carpenters, Mr. Hamilton, and anyway I am in something of a hurry because I planned to drive down to Tacoma today to attend an auction preview. I talked to the auction manager last night on the phone, and it sounds as though there might be several pieces you would like for your house. He has a kitchen table that came out of an old Port Townsend mansion, but then, they always claim everything came out of an old Port Townsend mansion, so I will believe it when I see it. He has a collection of rockers, too, and he swears he has a genuine American oak wardrobe, but I am skeptical, and also some brass pieces that might contain something unique that—"

"Is there some reason you don't want to go up to Birch House with me?" Mr. Hamilton interrupted.

"No! That is, if you're going up, I will go with you."

"I am going up," he said, and he sounded quite sure of his own decision.

Stacy nodded, grabbed her jacket, and followed him out to his car. It would be safer to go with him and explain. He would only see an unbelievable mess. She would have to explain how this mess would turn into a beautiful interior.

He drove in silence while Stacy rattled off descriptions of the wallpaper patterns that she had picked. If he heard or cared, he didn't say so.

They entered Birch House by pushing aside the black plastic curtain that Phillips had stapled over the doorway. He had removed the door to keep the glass from being broken by plaster when the wall was chipped away to expose a water pipe that had to be removed. Once inside, they stood ankle deep in debris. Stacy stopped talking and waited. Sometimes clients sobbed a bit at this point.

Mr. Hamilton looked around. "Looks like things are coming right along," he said.

Stacy started breathing again. "In another month you'll see a whole different house, Mr. Hamilton. We could go through the rooms now, and if you have any questions—"

They wandered from room to room. Stacy explained each change, its purpose and what it would eventually become, while Mr. Hamilton gazed and said nothing.

When they returned to the front hall, he said, "I do have one question, Miss Green."

"Yes?"

"This is a weekday morning, isn't it?"

"Yes."

"Then where are the workmen?"

"What? Oh. Oh, Mr. Hamilton, they're all paid by the hour. Mr. Phillips only charges you for the time they work. When they aren't here you aren't paying them, you see, so you don't—"

"I don't care about the explanations, I just want to know where they are."

Stacy glanced through the empty space where a window used to be at the bright sky and the sparkling water. She could tell him they were on another job, but she knew better. "Do you want the truth?" she said softly.

"Absolutely."

"I expect they're fishing."

"Fishing?"

"Mr. Hamilton, you don't want this house for another six months and tomorrow it might be raining. Phillips is a little short of work now, what with the recession and all, so he isn't pushing this job exactly, and when the weather is this good, well, I am afraid that when the sun shines, well—"

Mr. Hamilton interrupted her. "You mean the Islanders only work when it rains?"

"It rains a lot around here," Stacy said weakly.

To her surprise, he laughed.

She said, "If you're in a hurry, I will tell Phillips, and he'll keep his crew working weekends, but you did say—"

"No, don't do that. I am sure it will rain between now and August." He started back to the car and Stacy followed.

When they were driving down Sunday Hill, he said, "They're right. This is a rotten day to work. Where was that auction you wanted to preview?"

"Tacoma."

"Suppose I drive you down?"

"Would you?" Stacy cried. "I really would like you to go. They might have several things you could use, and I much prefer to have clients pick some of the key pieces."

"Why?"

"Because then it will be your house, not mine."

Stacy ran into the office to grab her purse and leave a note for Laura. Then she locked the door and joined Mr. Hamilton in his car. They caught the ferry to Seattle and drove south to Tacoma, one of her least favorite drives. Here civilization had pushed aside the trees, paved over the forest floors, and lined the whole road with neon signs, factories, tacky businesses, and airports. To the west the Cascades and some rebellious stands of fir insisted on rising above the man-made scenery, reminders of what lay outside the population centers. They were in Tacoma before noon.

At the auction showroom Stacy discovered that the wardrobe was all wrong for the house, but that one rocker would be perfect for the guest room, and several other pieces would work in other spots. Mr. Hamilton wandered off by himself through the showroom. When she caught up with him, she said, "If you like these things, I will leave written bids on them."

"Won't you come back and bid?"

"Not with someone else's money," she admitted. "I know what the pieces are worth; I'll bid that, but I won't go over. If we don't get them at that price, I will find them elsewhere."

"Miss Green, what is that thing?"

Stacy followed his gesture to a Belgian cook stove that burned wood and was covered with pale green ceramic tiles. Each tile was decorated with a white daisy design.

"It's a cooking stove. They come from Belgium or sometimes France."

"I like it."

"Yes. They come in all colors. Quite charming."

"I like *that* one," he said. "Didn't you say something about putting a wood-burning stove in the kitchen near the table?"

So he had listened to her. "Yes, I had in mind something of the Franklin stove type, rather as a fireplace substitute."

Stacy gazed at the stove, her eyes half-closed. "Umm. It is a nice shade. I could pick up the color elsewhere in the room. I am not quite sure of the dimensions, though. I hadn't begun to look for a stove yet and—"

Mr. Hamilton interrupted in a voice that Stacy realized he must use to end discussions at board meetings. "Make it fit. Knock out a wall and enlarge the kitchen if you have to. And you don't have to worry about the bid on it. I'll send one of my secretaries down here."

"It could go to two thousand," Stacy warned.

"He'll pay whatever he has to," Mr. Hamilton said. "Is there anything else you want?"

"I think that's all. Most of the things here are much too formal for your house."

"Then let's get out of here and find some place for lunch. I have to get back to Seattle for a meeting this afternoon."

"Don't be late on my account," Stacy said politely. "I can eat later."

"I can't," he said, and his tone left no room for discussion. He slipped his hand under her elbow and guided her firmly but courteously out of the gallery to his car.

Stacy would have been satisfied with a drive-in or a coffee shop, but apparently that idea never entered Mr. Hamilton's head. He took her to a restaurant that Stacy could only describe as "plush," and they lunched on filet mignon and cracked crab.

"I am really pleased that you picked the Belgian stove," Stacy told him over her wineglass.

"You think it suits the house?"

"If we were doing an historical reconstruction for a museum, no, but we're not. We're planning a vacation house for you and, up to now, none of my plans have reflected your taste because I didn't know what it was. So I am delighted to have a major piece that you picked yourself."

He leaned back. "Miss Green, are you saying the

stove represents something of the bad taste of the owner, which every house should have?"

"Oh, no! I didn't mean that at all! I think the stove has real charm. Besides, Miss Rouse said she wanted some unique items, and that stove is exactly the sort of item *Homes of Distinction* likes to feature."

"Homes of Distinction?" This time she had forced him to break his poker face. His eyebrows rose in surprise.

"Why, yes, that is, you know, the magazine. . . ." Stacy's voice trailed off. Miss Rouse had been so specific. Had Mr. Hamilton not wanted Stacy to know about the magazine?

"The magazine? *Homes of Distinction?* What about it?"

"But—I—Miss Rouse said—"

He waited, not speaking, and let Stacy flounder.

"She, uh, when she came by to see me, and then again, oh, she mentioned that the house was to be photographed for *Homes of Distinction*. Therefore she was especially interested in the accuracy of the decoration, and also that, well, there should be some unique pieces, the sort of thing *Homes of Distinction* likes."

He stared at her for what seemed like hours, but could only have been seconds. Even that was too much. Silences in conversations drove Stacy wild.

"Didn't you know?" she blurted. "I assumed that of course you and she had planned this together. I mean, Mr. Hamilton, you yourself told me the house should have charm and uniqueness, and that is what Miss Rouse said. So naturally I thought—"

He waved his hand at her in a silencing gesture and Stacy realized she had been talking too loudly. Embarrassed, she stopped.

He leaned toward her and said softly, "It's all right, Miss Green. Don't be upset. I had no idea why Dominic wanted that house or why she had such strange ideas about the redecorating. So, what I told you was simply what she had told me. It made no difference to me how we decorated the place. A house on the Island was Dominic's idea, which is quite all right, and it seemed an interesting idea, a change from our other homes which are mainly in cities, but I suppose she forgot to mention the magazine. She has a friend who is connected with the magazine in some way. Well, now I understand why she wanted the house photographed before the remodeling."

For once, Stacy ran out of words. She stared back at him, her black eyes wide in her small face.

He hesitated, then added, "Dominic likes to think up little projects. Would you like your coffee now?"

"Yes, please." As she could think of nothing else to say, Stacy glanced around the table for something to do to fill the silence. The idea of Birch House being a little project, a layout in *Homes of Distinction,* so unimportant that it need not be mentioned, completely rattled her. Actually, she could think of about a thousand things to say, but none of them seemed to be either polite or any of her business. What sort of relationship did he have with this Miss Rouse that he bought her houses as hobbies and spent thousands of dollars on them to amuse her? What did he mean by "our other homes"? How many homes did he have? Who was "our"? He and Miss Rouse weren't married yet. Perhaps he meant future homes when he said that. With so many questions blurring her thinking, Stacy reached for her wineglass, felt instinctively that she really didn't want wine, switched her choice to the water glass, and managed to knock both of them over.

Mr. Hamilton's reflexes were fast but not fast enough. He caught and uprighted both glasses after their contents had rushed over the edge of the tablecloth onto his pants legs. He made some sort of motion with his hand, a waiter flurried around them, the glasses were removed, the pants dabbed dry, and while Stacy sat immobile, dying of embarrassment, Mr. Hamilton said to the waiter, "I believe the lady would like her coffee now."

When the waiter had served coffee and disappeared, Mr. Hamilton said softly, "Please don't hurry with the coffee. I would rather have it slowly in you than quickly on me."

"Oh, Mr. Hamilton! I *am* sorry."

"No, don't apologize. It is quite all right. Just surprising. For some reason I assumed decorators would be people with good reflexes, what with handling fragile objects so much and that sort of thing."

"I don't suppose Miss Rouse ever spills anything!" Stacy blurted, then clapped her hand over her mouth. What had possessed her to say that? She would have liked to slide right under the table and disappear.

To her surprise, he laughed. "No, she doesn't," he said. "She never falls off ladders on people, either. Too bad, because I find it rather appealing. I must tell Dominic to learn to be a bit more clumsy."

"Oh, honestly. I feel so stupid."

"Then I shouldn't tease you."

Searching about for a change of topic, which she felt was desperately needed, Stacy finally said, "Mr. Hamilton, could I ask you a question? It's none of my business, and it is asked purely out of curiosity so I suppose it is a rude question, but you mentioned something about several homes, and I was, well, wondering. What sort of homes do you have? I mean, the word 'several.' That is, most people would say 'my other house,' or 'my other two houses,' or something like that."

"I don't have other houses. It's because of the business, you see. My family has hotels around the world, and so we have apartments in each hotel reserved for any of us all the time. They aren't *my* apartments. My brother and my uncle and my parents use them also, but we aren't all in the same one at the same time. They aren't really homes, for that matter, but when I'm living out of a suitcase, I try to avoid the suitcase feeling. So I leave clothes in each one and try to think of them as homes rather than two-week stops."

"I see."

"My parents have a house on Long Island and one in Florida. That's all." He said it as though the houses were tract homes with wall-to-wall neighbors, but Stacy visualized estates surrounded by manicured gardens and filled with servants and she knew instinctively that she was right. "Probably Dominic and I will have a permanent home in the East," he continued. "We've been looking, but we haven't found quite what we want."

"I suppose your work keeps you on the East Coast most of the time."

"Not especially. But that's where our families are. Dominic's father's law office is in New York."

"You have a very exciting life," Stacy sighed. "All that travel."

"Do you think so? Sometimes I feel that my real home is an airplane seat. You'd be surprised how boring airplane interiors can be. And now that you know all about me, Miss Green, tell me about you. It's only fair. How many homes do you have? Are you engaged? Who is this Tom you are always mentioning?"

"Oh! Tom is a painting contractor and he's working on your house. He is an old school friend, I mean, really old, all the way back to first grade. No, I am not engaged, and when it comes to homes, I have two, an apartment which I share with Laura Leitzel and an office which I share with Laura Leitzel. Or I could count my car and that makes three."

"This Tom isn't the marrying kind?"

"Tom?" Stacy gathered up her purse and jacket as the waiter held her chair for her. "Yes, indeed. Soon. You won't be late to your meeting, will you?"

"I can't be. It starts when I get there," he said.

Did he snap his fingers and tell the world when to start each morning? Stacy wondered.

He offered to take the ferry to the Island with her, but she said, of course not; her office was only a short walk from the ferry dock. It would be a waste of time for him to make the round trip.

"And after a while the ferry rides are about as exciting as your plane trips," she said.

"There is much nicer scenery from the ferry," he assured her as he pulled up to the curb and let her out at the Seattle dock.

She thanked him, then watched his car pull into the

traffic. By the time she returned to the office, Laura had gone home and returned with Priscilla.

"Off running around again," Laura teased. "What sort of business are we running with no one at the phone? Speaking of phones, Tom has been phoning. Wanted to know if you'd placed the wallpaper order. I assured him you had. You have, haven't you?"

"Of course."

"And the dentist—"

"Don't tell me. There are so many snags on that job. I'll stop by and see him."

"How was the auction preview?"

Stacy scratched Priscilla's ears. Priscilla glared at her. "Why can't you purr like other cats?" Stacy asked. "The auction was interesting. Found some suitable items. Mr. Hamilton went with me."

"*The* handsome, breathtaking Mr. Hamilton?"

"Himself."

"Accompanied, no doubt, by the fabulous Miss Rouse?"

"All by ourselves. Lucky you weren't in the office or you probably would have offered to chaperone us."

"Yes, indeed," Laura agreed.

"And that would have ruined your diet. He took me to lunch at a very elegant place with a million waiters and a simple menu of filet mignon and cracked crab."

"Don't! You're torturing me! I hope the fantastic Mr. Hamilton was his usual brusque, boorish self and rushed you through the meal and refused to speak so that you had to carry on the conversation all by yourself."

"It's funny, he's not like that at all now that I know him better. He is really very nice. I spilled my wine and water all over his suit and he ordered me a cup of coffee."

"He wanted to give you another shot?" Laura demanded.

Stacy laughed. "Also, for the first time he had an opinion about the house. He picked out a piece for the kitchen and I was really pleased about that. I have never before had a client with no choices, and I live in dread that when Birch House is all done, he will walk in the door, take one look and say, 'I hate the whole thing.' "

"With his money, he could afford to have you do it over."

"That's not the point. I don't want to take advantage of him simply because he can afford it. I'm not in this business just to make money, Laura."

Laura winced. "I hope you won't tell the bank that. They phoned today about an overdraft."

"That's impossible! I deposited Mr. Hamilton's check!"

"For once you're right and they're wrong. I found their error."

Stacy let out her breath and sank into her chair.

"Don't relax that fast. We're nearing the bottom of the Hamilton check because we've been paying off bills on the dentist's office and the Adams place."

"I'll stop and see both of them today and collect something. Don't pay any more of their bills. If they won't pay in, we'll reroute the bills to them or something, but that Hamilton money has to be there for Tom's salary. I'll get another estimate off to Mr. Hamilton and—oh, I am sick of money."

"Where *was* Miss Rouse today?" Laura asked. "I'm asking that to change the subject and also because I'm curious."

"He didn't say. He did mention that he's flying back to New York tomorrow so I suppose she didn't come with him. He won't be back until the first of May, and I hope that by then Phillips will have replaced what he's ripped out."

"What's the hurry?"

"Tom. There's only two rooms he can work in until Phillips gets done and Tom needs the work now. He and Angie want to get married soon."

She thought of Tom and Angie; he was as big and clumsy as Angie was small and graceful. They complemented each other. As long as Stacy could remember, they had been a pair, chasing each other home from grade school, holding hands in high school. How nice to have someone you loved that much, someone you shared your whole life with, all your thoughts and memories, all your worries and joys. It must give them both a wonderful sense of belonging. They were as much a part of the community as the fir trees.

Stacy had never had that sort of relationship with any of the boys at school. Oh, she had dated, as did everyone, and there had been guys she liked and guys she didn't like, but no one special, no one who meant anything to her, no one with whom she wanted to go past the hand-holding stage. A few had tried to get serious, but she simply hadn't cared for them. And it wasn't that she didn't want to care. She didn't hate boys. She didn't want to remain single. On the other hand, she didn't want to marry just to be marrying. He had to be the right man. Stacy was beginning to think that Mr. Right didn't exist.

"Speaking of Tom," Laura said, "he wanted you to call him."

Stacy reached for the phone and dialed his number. "Tom? Laura said you called."

"Yes, sorry to bother you, Stacy, but I wanted to be sure you had those orders in. Also, I'm going to start bugging Phillips to get the upstairs finished first so that I can get in there, if that's okay with you."

"Good luck. I can never get him to hurry."

"If I stand over his carpenters, they'll move in the direction I want. I'm going to start on the back bedroom floors tomorrow so I'll be right there. They'll get sick of me pestering."

"That's all right, Tom, do whatever you want."

"I want to get the whole job done by June first."

"Oh? Super. You and Angie have set a wedding date then?"

"I'd like to—I want to leave then. How soon can you pay me off?"

"There shouldn't be any problem on this job, Tom. I'm sure I can give you your money as soon as you turn in time sheets. Where are you going?"

"I don't know. Away. Any place."

He didn't sound happy, but Stacy asked, "A surprise honeymoon, huh? Sounds very romantic."

"No, Angie isn't going with me. The wedding is off."

"What?"

"It's off, that's all. I don't want to talk about it right now."

"Oh. Of course. I'm sorry. You do what you like about the house, Tom. I'll be out there tomorrow."

"All right. I'll see you then."

He hung up, and Stacy sat at her desk staring at the receiver. What did he mean, the wedding was off? Stacy felt betrayed. Here she had visualized Tom and Angie as the ideal romance, the perfect marriage, and now they had let her down. When "the perfect-couple" movie stars split up, Stacy was never surprised because she never expected those glamor marriages to work, anyway. But Tom and Angie? They were as solid as Mt. Rainier, as traditional as the St. Patrick's Day parade in Seattle, as stable as—as—oh, she couldn't think what. Might as well tell her Puget Sound had run out of saltwater.

"It won't ring if you keep it in your hand," Laura said.

Slowly, Stacy replaced the receiver. "Tom and Angie aren't getting married," she said.

"Who can afford to?"

"No, I mean they've—something is wrong. Tom wants to leave town. Without Angie."

Laura's mouth dropped. She grabbed her phone and dialed. "My cousin should—hello, Susan? Laura. Hey, what's the deal on Tom and Angie? She did? No, I only heard . . . uh-huh. Okay, see you."

As Laura hung up the phone, Stacy said pleasantly, "One of the nice things about this island is the complete privacy everyone enjoys."

Laura's round face dimpled. "Do you want to hear or don't you?"

"All right, tell me."

"Tom and Angie had a terrible fight but Angie wouldn't say what it was about. She called Susan last night and asked her to drive her to the ferry. She said she was taking a bus to Vancouver to visit an aunt, and she didn't want Tom to know where she was going because she never wanted to see him again as long as she lived."

"That's terrible."

"Yes, Susan thought so. She tried to talk Angie out of leaving, but you know how stubborn Angie can be, and she insisted she could not stay any longer as she never wanted to lay eyes on Tom again. And, of course, she has a point. It is not possible to remain on this island and count on not seeing any one particular person. Unless maybe you move into a tree house and never come down. And even then, the very person you don't want to see will probably come crawling up, chasing his cat. So there you are."

"Susan didn't know what the argument was about?"

"No. I guess it was a lulu."

So much for love, Stacy thought. If Tom and Angie couldn't make a go of it, who could? She thought she would never believe in romance or happy marriages again.

Chapter Five

April rained itself away. Stacy barely had time to think about it. She raced in and out of the office between downpours and somehow finally completed the dentist's office and the Adams job. Along with all the other miracles of spring, both accounts were paid in full by the first of May. Laura picked up several small jobs which kept her busy.

Besides the pleasure of being paid for the other two jobs, Stacy had Birch House. Each time she looked at it she felt the twinges of spring fever. Phillips had completed the upstairs and exterior and now concentrated on the main floor. Willy's Green Thumb Service, which consisted of Willy, his nephew, and neighborhood teenagers paid by the hour, had cleared away all the weeds and blackberry tangles and reset the picket fence. Most of the pickets were beyond repair so old Ed Gordon, who did odd jobs when his arthritis wasn't bothering him, replaced the pickets, built new gates, and painted the whole fence.

On the first day of May, Stacy buried her account books in the file and drove out to Birch House. She parked across the road, climbed out of the car, and stood soaking in the unexpected sunshine and the picture-book prettiness that had emerged from the neglected jumble. Birch House shone white under its new red roof. Freed from the weeds, an enormous old rose-bush rambled down the side fence, carefully pruned and retied by Willy and Ed. Small green buds promised later glory. The cherry tree was an umbrella of white blossoms above the gravel patio at one side of the house, and Ed had built an octagonal bench around

63

its dark trunk. In the front garden, on either side of the new gravel paths that led to the door, Willy had uncovered mounds of blue Scilla, long lost under weeds. Forget-me-nots surrounded the white birches and pale new birch leaves shimmered in the sun. Every empty spot was filled with the green shoots of annuals and perennials, lovingly chosen by Stacy and Willy to match the old garden.

In front of the new, enlarged kitchen window, the French lilac had burst into enormous lavender clusters, and in back of the house the dusty red flowers of Paul Scarlett hawthorne spilled over the hedge of Bridal Wreath. Willy had not yet cleared the backyard because Phillips' carpenters were still using it as a dumping ground for their materials.

Stacy wandered slowly up the path to the front door. By the new brick steps Willy had placed an old wooden tub of yellow tulips. Stacy opened the front door and stepped from paradise into chaos. Only the walls in the parlor had been replaced and Tom had not yet begun to paint and paper. The entry was a jumble of old boards and plaster and torn walls. The dining room was even worse. Stacy ducked through it to the kitchen, then gasped. She had not been to Birch House in a week, and she had definitely not been prepared for miracles. Tom turned on his heels and grinned at her. He was squatting down by the sink, replacing a hinge on a cabinet door.

When she had last seen the room, it was almost as awful as the front hall, except that the appliances had been installed and the cabinet backs built. Now the walls had been papered, the lovely old wooden doors had been hung on the cabinets, and the dark red cedar floors were shining. In the corner stood the tile stove. Outside, the lilac bush pressed against the window.

"All we need to do is bring in the rug and furniture from the barn," Tom said.

"Oh, Tom, it's gorgeous! You are an absolute magician!"

"You made the choices, Stacy. All I did was provide the muscle."

"No, that's not true. You're a real artist, Tom."

Tom walked over and dropped his arm around her shoulders in a friendly hug. She slid her arm around his waist, unconsciously hugging him back as they gazed together in complete satisfaction at the riot of lilac clusters and the cheerful little stove.

The kitchen door opened behind them. They heard it and looked around slowly, assuming it was one of Phillips' men. Instead, framed in the doorway were Mr. Hamilton and Miss Rouse.

"Good morning," Tom said cheerfully, his arm dropping away from Stacy.

"How nice to see you again, Miss Green," Miss Rouse said, her perfect smile flashing in her lovely face. "We seem to have just missed you at your office."

"I'm glad you came on out," Stacy said, hurrying over to them. "This is Tom Barrows, our painting contractor. He's a genius, really, and I know you're going to love what he's done."

Miss Rouse slid into the kitchen. Stacy couldn't quite think of any other way to describe the smooth, flowing motion which seemed to have nothing to do with putting one foot in front of the other. Or perhaps Miss Rouse floated. Mr. Hamilton, on the other hand, definitely walked. His step was as firm as his personality. Without saying a word, he turned and observed every inch of the kitchen.

"It's charming, truly charming," Miss Rouse gushed, "and you must tell me something about the history of that wallpaper pattern. And, oh, what is that?" She pointed at the stove.

"It's a cook stove. They were made in Belgium and the tiles are in excellent condition. Of course, there's an electric stove built into the cabinets over there for actual cooking, but this can be used to warm the corner and add atmosphere. It burns wood."

"The rest of the room is lovely," Miss Rouse said, "but personally, I can't stand that stove. Please have it removed."

Mr. Hamilton said, "I picked out the stove."

Embarrassed, Stacy rattled, "You did say you wanted

some unique pieces, you know, collector's items, Miss Rouse, and that stove really is unique. You simply won't see another like it, not the exact same tile pattern and—"

Mr. Hamilton's voice was flat. He cut Stacy off. "I picked it because I like it. It stays."

Miss Rouse flashed the smile that had brightened her marriage-announcement photograph. "Oh, darling, it is quaint, it really is, it's only that I wasn't sure it fit *there*, but if you like it there, then of course we'll leave it."

"The garden is coming along nicely," Mr. Hamilton said.

"Isn't it?" Stacy said. "The gardener is a genius. Now you must go upstairs and see what Tom has done."

"Oh, yes, let's see the upstairs," Miss Rouse said. "Is it furnished?"

"No, but most of the furniture is in the barn, waiting to be moved in. The carpenters are still working in the downstairs."

"Are they?" Mr. Hamilton asked, looking through the kitchen door and across the dining room to the front hall.

Stacy had no idea why Tom was alone in the house, but she refrained from mentioning the possibility of fishing. When Mr. Hamilton marched into the parlor to inspect the new doors, Miss Rouse dropped back and said softly, "Miss Green, are you sure that stove is all right in there? I mean, it looks odd to me."

"I think the arrangement should work very well," Stacy said. "It's completely out of the traffic pattern so it won't be in your way for cooking or serving—"

"I don't mean that," Miss Rouse said. "I don't cook. I never go in the kitchen. I mean, it doesn't look like much. That is, is it really a unique piece?"

"It is quite valuable," Stacy said, "and fairly rare."

"You know, I think it would be better if you picked out the rest of the furnishings. Avery doesn't—his taste sometimes—that is, I would prefer that you do it yourself."

And what did she think Stacy could do if Mr. Hamilton picked a piece and had it delivered? He was paying. It was his house. Stacy said, "I'm sure you'll like everything else."

Miss Rouse sighed, but somehow it was a theatrical sigh, sounding as though she had practiced it. "It's a pity I haven't had time to do any of the shopping for the house but I have been so busy. You can't imagine the problems that come up in planning a wedding. So many details."

"Yes, of course. You must be getting excited now with such a marvelous honeymoon trip planned. How I would love to spend a summer in Europe."

"Would you? I suppose so. I'd rather stay at one of the beach resorts, but Avery insists we sightsee in Greece. I hope it won't be too hot."

"How marvelous! All those temples!"

"Oh, the temples. I've seen those in Italy. They are really a bore. Nothing but piles of old stones."

They picked their way across old boards to the entry. Stacy explained her plans for each area, but Miss Rouse didn't seem particularly interested. She nodded and said, "That's nice," in a bored tone. Stacy felt deflated. Surely such a gorgeous wedding gift as Birch House deserved a little more enthusiasm. Still, she supposed a woman who was bored by temples wouldn't be too excited by a cherry tree in bloom or a description of an antique wardrobe.

They followed Avery Hamilton and Tom upstairs to inspect the bedrooms. It was like entering another world. Here the woodwork and floors gleamed their rich, natural colors, and the walls were papered in light flower patterns. The new bathroom fixtures were in place.

"Looks done," Mr. Hamilton said.

"Yes, all it needs is some cleaning up of the windows. Then we'll be ready to move in the furnishings, but we won't until Phillips is done downstairs. I prefer to get him out since we really can't lock up the house with his men coming and going."

To herself Stacy wondered desperately where Phillips and his men were. If only the sound of pounding

were echoing through the house, how much more con-
vinced Mr. Hamilton would be that they were earning
their price.

Then Miss Rouse said it. "Where are the carpenters?"
she asked innocently.

Before Stacy could answer, Mr. Hamilton said pleasantly, "We came on a sunny day, Dominic. That's the
problem. Islanders don't work on sunny days."

Miss Rouse purred, "How quaint. Whyever not?"

"I—uh, we haven't hung the light fixture above the
stairs, and you really must see it," Stacy said rapidly,
pulling open the closet door where the fixture was
stashed and taking it out. It was a long metal rod that
would hang several feet under the ceiling when it was
installed and would support a wreath of scrollwork and
fluted lamp shade bases.

Stacy followed Mr. Hamilton out of the bedroom to
the top of the stairs while Tom and Miss Rouse lingered
in the master bedroom. Tom was pointing out the cedar
floors.

"I only found it last week," Stacy hurried on, her
words tumbling over each other to avoid any silent
gaps that could lead to a discussion of Island workers
who fished on sunny days, "and it is really unusual, but
perhaps of more interest is that it came out of the old
Sidney Hotel at—"

As she spoke, she swung around with the fixture in
her hands, and the rod struck Mr. Hamilton squarely
across the chest.

Stacy screamed. Mr. Hamilton groped wildly, teetered
on the top step, and tried futilely to catch the balustrade. Then, as Stacy rushed toward him, his tall form
snapped forward, then collapsed backward instead.

Stacy dropped the fixture. It clattered on the bare
floor.

The whole house shuddered as Mr. Hamilton slid
upside-down on his back the length of the stairs. At
least, it seemed to Stacy as though the house shuddered.
With a screech she rushed down after him, tripped on
the bottom step, and sprawled across him on the plaster-
strewn entry floor.

"Avery!" Miss Rouse called. "Are you all right?"

Beneath her, Mr. Hamilton said softly, "Can you please get off me, Miss Green?"

Stacy pushed herself back and knelt beside him. "Oh, I am so—Mr. Hamilton!"

His face was drawn into a pinched expression of extreme pain. She knew immediately that the only reason he wasn't screaming was that he was not the sort of man who would ever allow himself to scream.

"What is it?" she cried.

"I—I think—I think my leg is broken. I can't be sure."

"Don't move!" Stacy cried.

"I hadn't planned to," he whispered and passed out. His eyes closed, and his face went dead white.

"Oh, my God," Stacy gasped.

Tom pounded down the stairs behind her, peered at Mr. Hamilton, touched his throat, then said, "Stacy, I'll run next door to the phone and get the aid car. You stay here. Don't touch him."

Next door was a quarter of a mile down the road, but Stacy didn't argue. With no phone in Birch House, there was nothing else to do.

Miss Rouse came down the stairs and leaned over Stacy, then let out a gasp. "What's wrong with him?"

"He's fainted. I'm afraid he's broken his leg."

"Broken his leg! That's impossible. Avery! Avery!" She leaned over him, calling his name, and the whole scene seemed totally unreal to Stacy, as though she were watching a TV show. She knew that she should do something or say something, but she could think of nothing. Instead, she knelt by him, staring at his white face, while his fiancée called his name and wrung her hands. What if something terrible were wrong with him, something more than a broken leg? Suppose his back were broken?

It was her fault! He could lie here on the littered floor of the half-remodeled house and die of shock, and it would be all her fault.

Her mind snapped back to reality. Vaguely she remembered a point she had learned in a first-aid class in high school. If there were a danger of shock, it was important to keep the victim warm. Neither she nor Miss Rouse were wearing coats, and she dared not move Mr. Hamilton to draw his coat around him. Wildly she tried to remember what she might have in her car. Then she remembered a box of quilts stored in the barn, marvelous old handmade quilts that she had bought from a dealer and planned to display on a quilt rack in the guest bedroom.

"Don't touch him," she warned Miss Rouse, and then ran out to the barn. By the time she found the box among the stacks of stored furniture, she was surprised to realize that she was saying aloud, over and over, "Please don't die. Please don't die."

She clamped her mouth on the words, knowing she must not voice them in front of Miss Rouse. She felt tears on her cheeks but could not remember crying. She brushed them away with a dusty hand, dug an armful of quilts from the box and rushed back to the house.

While she explained about keeping shock victims warm, she spread the quilts over Mr. Hamilton, careful not to touch him when she tucked them in. The possibility that his back was broken numbed her mind with terror. "That is right, isn't it?" she said, trying to sound cheerful. "You do cover shock victims?"

"I—I think I heard—I don't know, really," Miss Rouse said. "How—what—how did Avery fall?"

Stacy pressed her hands into her face and whispered, "I—I feel so terrible—I don't know how I could have— oh, it's all my fault." She would have burst into tears, but the aid car sirens brought her mind out of her own fears.

Within minutes firemen from the volunteer department swarmed around Mr. Hamilton, spoke back and forth to each other, moved Stacy gently out of the way, and then stepped back for the doctor. Stacy watched wide eyed from the doorway, her eyes bright with tears.

Steady hands lifted the long form from the floor, settled it gently onto a stretcher, and carried it out of the house. As they passed her, Mr. Hamilton's eyes opened, stared straight into hers, and then closed again. His still, white face looked so dead that when she saw his eyes move she could almost have shouted with relief.

When the aid car had gone, with Miss Rouse inside it with her fiancé, Stacy stood on the front steps staring down the hill.

Tom put his arm around her. "Hey, he's going to be all right."

"Oh, Tom! I could have killed him!"

"You? What do you mean, you?"

"I—I knocked him down the stairs."

"What? When I saw you, you were lying on top of him. What happened, anyway?"

"I was showing him the light fixture, and I swung around and hit him with it; he lost his balance and I ran after him to help him, and I tripped on the bottom stair and, oh, Tom, I could have killed him!"

"Hey, hey, slow down," Tom said softly. "It sounds like something only you could do, but he isn't going to die, Stace. Honest. The doc said his leg was broken. That's all. He isn't going to die from a broken leg."

Suddenly all the fear, all the wild thoughts, all the emotions that she had fought so hard to control in front of Miss Rouse welled up in Stacy, and she burst into tears. Sobbing, she covered her face. Tom pulled her into his arms. She heard him telling her to go ahead and cry. There was no way that she could stop crying so she did just that. Finally the sobs died down of their own accord and she pushed herself back from Tom to apologize.

He pulled out an enormous handkerchief and started to dab at the tears on her face. She took it from him, grinned through her tears, and wiped her own face. Tom was such a big man, tall and broad and heavy, that he made her feel like a tiny child.

"I'm all right, now."

"You want me to drive you back to town?"

"No, of course not. I need my car."

"I could bring you back out to get it."

"Don't be silly. I'm all right. Really. Only it was all

such a shock." Stacy's hand shook as she handed him his handkerchief, but she bit her lip to hold back any further tears.

"Sure, Stace. All right then, I'll stay here a while and get a little more work done."

"I think I had better get back to the office so that I can phone the doctor and—and the hospital. I—I have to know if Mr. Hamilton is going to be all right."

Tom placed one large hand under Stacy's small, pointed chin, tipped her face up, and looked straight into her eyes. He said slowly, "You really care about him, don't you?"

"You'd care, too, if you knocked a client down the stairs and broke his leg!"

"No, I don't mean that. And you know it. Be careful, Stacy, don't break your heart over that guy. He isn't your type."

Stacy's black eyes flashed. "Why, Tom, that's the dumbest thing I ever heard! I am not the least bit—I mean, really, he is just a client, and I can't imagine why . . ." Her voice trailed off.

Tom dropped his hand from her face and shrugged. "Yeah, sure, it is pretty dumb, isn't it, me telling you how to handle your love life when I can't even keep track of my own."

"Oh, Tom!" As he turned away from her, Stacy touched his arm. "Haven't you heard anything from Angie?"

"I don't want to talk about it," he said and disappeared inside the house.

Stacy stood on the front steps, staring out across the tops of the fir trees to the distant water. A white dot that she knew was a gull circled slowly above the blue surface. Even here, high on Sunday Hill, she could smell the sea, its sharp odor mingling with the fragrance of the blossoming cherry tree.

Something cold enveloped her heart. Fear. She told herself that she was shaking because she had been through a terrible fright. Even now, she had no way of knowing if Mr. Hamilton would recover quickly and completely from his fall. No one would know how serious his injuries might be until he reached the hospital and was x-rayed. That alone was enough to terrify anyone.

If there were other shadows on her heart, she could not admit it. She was sure that her fear for him was no greater than it would be for anyone else she might have knocked down the stairs. Stacy smiled involuntarily at that thought. Fortunately, she could not compare how she felt about his accident with any past experience because, although she did tend to be clumsy, she had never before sent anyone hurtling backwards down a flight of stairs.

She hurried down to her car and carefully drove back to town. First she would call the doctor's office and leave a message for him.

When she reached the office, she found it empty. A note on her desk from Laura said that she was out on a call. Stacy dialed the clinic.

"No, Doctor went over to Seattle with the ambulance, Stacy," the nurse told her. "I haven't heard from him. Let's see, the ferry should be docking about now, so I think it will be at least another hour before he knows anything."

"If he phones you, Mary, will you call me?"

"Of course. Was this Mr. Hamilton a friend of yours?"

"A client. He fell in a house I am decorating for him."

"Oh, dear. I see. Well, Doctor phoned from the dock on this side before the ferry left to tell me to cancel his afternoon appointments, and he said then that he thought it was only a broken leg, although there was a possibility of concussion. But he didn't sound particularly worried so I'm sure the patient will be all right."

"Still, he thought it was serious enough to take him to the hospital! I mean, he could set a broken leg in the office, couldn't he?"

"I—I think he wanted complete X-rays and, really, I wouldn't worry, if I were you."

Stacy thanked her and hung up. Saying not to worry was easy to do but hard to follow. Stacy knew that the local clinic had an X-ray machine. They could X-ray a broken leg. Did the doctor suspect a back injury? Internal injuries? What was that about a concussion? Would Mr. Hamilton need surgery?

Stacy bit hard on her finger. Tears threatened beneath her eyelids. She saw in her mind the crumpled form at the bottom of the stairs, felt the warm body as she sprawled across him, and then with a shock of pain, remembered the way he had looked at her, his gray eyes dull in his white face. What had he said? Something odd.

He'd said, "Can you please get off me, Miss Green?"

How could he! He had been rigid with pain; she knew that now. No doubt that was why he had lost consciousness. Then how could he have gone through that "Please, Miss Green" routine? Perhaps he had been in shock, even then. Yet he had said it as though they were total strangers, as though they'd never lunched together or—or—Stacy's mind stopped. For a moment she had thought of him as a friend, someone who had shared his thoughts with her, but that wasn't true. She knew nothing of his thoughts. Always, he had kept their conversations so impersonal that she had been forced to guess at his likes and dislikes. She had even had to learn his marriage plans from a newspaper! Wouldn't an ordinary man have told her, that first day, that he would be married in June, wanted the house decorated as a wedding gift for his fiancée, and would like to have it done by August when they returned from their honeymoon? Anyone else would have done that.

Or would they? Certainly. Stacy turned over in her thoughts all her clients and all the personal things they had told her. Yes, but most of them were Island neighbors and thought of themselves as her friends, which they were. This Mr. Hamilton was something different, popping in from a world that had never touched her own. Perhaps, in his world, people did not confide in those with whom they did business. Or was it just him? Dominic Rouse had told Stacy all about her plans to have the house photographed. She had given Stacy quite a peek into her world.

Stacy ruffled through papers on her desk, rearranged

the files and sorted mail, her mind never quite on her tasks. When the phone finally rang, she very nearly knocked it out of its cradle when she grabbed it.

"Stacy, this is Mary at the clinic. Doctor just phoned and I wanted to let you know. Your client has a broken leg, all right, and multiple bruises, but no concussion and no back injury. I asked specifically because I knew you were worried."

"Will he be all right?"

"He won't be dancing for some time, dearie, but on the other hand, we only shoot horses."

"Oh, Mary! What an awful thing to say. And you a nurse!"

Mary laughed. "I'm sorry. I see a parade of broken legs during ski season, and they really are awful for the patient, but that's because of the boredom, not the pain. The best thing you can do for our Mr. Hamilton is to find him some good books and stop in to visit him. He'll be in the hospital for a few days. After that, he'll be stuck in a chair somewhere with his leg up and lots of time to go batty."

"You're sure that's all?"

"Yes, and I have another call coming in. 'Bye, Stacy."

Stacy hung up the phone and was surprised to find herself shaking violently. He was all right. He wasn't crippled for life, or about to die, or any of the horrible things she had feared and tried to push out of her mind. Stacy pushed away the papers on her desk and buried her head in her folded arms. At least now she could relax.

Whether Mr. Hamilton would have more to say on the subject later was another matter. Was she liable? Would he sue her? Probably she would be responsible for his hospital bills. She would have to wait and see. If she were, it could wipe out the business but just now she couldn't care. All that mattered was that he was all right. At last, she could admit to herself how terrified she had been.

The phone rang again.

"Yes?"

Laura's voice said, "Stacy, we have a little problem."

"What?"

"Angie's here. At the apartment. She doesn't want Tom to know she's back on the Island. So she wants to stay with us but can she do that without him finding out?"

"Angie? I—all right, I suppose so, only—Laura, why don't I lock up now and come home? I've had a rotten day."

Laura said slowly, "Don't come here to get cheered up, my girl. You could float a battleship in the tears."

Stacy lowered the receiver, gathered her purse and keys, hung the closed sign in the window, and headed for home. She couldn't think of anything more she could accomplish today short of running over a fire truck.

Chapter Six

Angie was curled up in the one large chair in the apartment. If the Creator had set out to design an exact opposite to Tom, he succeeded when he designed Angie. She was small and delicate, with an upturned nose and neat dark hair that curled up at the ends. Only her eyes matched Tom's in color, a bright blue, but while his eyes were surrounded by short, stiff blond lashes, her eyes were shadowed by long dark crescents. For all her lack of size, she had ten times Tom's temper. Where he moved slowly, spoke softly, and reminded Stacy of a teddy bear, Angie crackled like a flame.

"You won't tell Tom that I'm here," she demanded again.

Stacy said, "That's a little hard, Ange. I see Tom every few days."

"I'm not asking you to lie to him. Just don't mention me."

"Why is that so important?"

"I don't want to see him, that's all! If he knows I'm here, he'll be coming around. I know Tom."

"And what about your parents?"

"They think I'm still in Vancouver."

"Angie! You can't hide out forever."

"Am I in your way?"

"No, of course not, but someone is sure to see you eventually. What's all the secrecy, anyway?"

"You can't understand," Angie said. "See, you've never been in love."

Stacy winced.

"It's awful, just awful, and I wish I had never been

in love, either, or at least, not with Tom. That big, dumb ape, he isn't worth it, he really isn't."

Stacy thought of Tom and the way he had comforted her when Mr. Hamilton fell, and the times he had let her owe him money. She could say a thousand things in his defense, but she didn't know what to defend. Finally she said, "I wish I were in love with someone like Tom. My life would be much simpler."

"No, it wouldn't," Angie flared. "Do you know how long I have been going with that clown? Fourteen years! That's right! Since first grade, Stacy, and wouldn't you think that's long enough for an engagement? Wouldn't you think he'd be ready to get married?"

Stacy protested, "But Tom said you were going to marry in June."

"Oh, yes. June. *If* he gets his way. Well, he won't, and that is that. I won't marry such a baboon."

"If he gets his way about what? No, you don't have to tell me," Stacy added quickly. "It's none of my business and I shouldn't have asked."

"Then tell *me*," Laura interrupted. "I am going out of my gourd wondering what you're up to, Angie."

Angie chewed thoughtfully on a ragged fingernail. "I might as well tell you. Then you'll know why I have to hide out. See, Tom thinks we don't have enough money to get married, and he is right, we don't. Not on his salary. But I was making good money at the bank so I figured with our two incomes we could make it, right? So we agreed on June. Mind you, this is only the third time we've set a date. So then, when I thought everything was settled, Tom says, 'Be sure to give notice at your job in May.' Can you believe that? 'Why?' I asked, and that dope says, 'You don't think I'd let my wife work, do you?' Honestly, if that isn't right out of the Dark Ages!"

"And that's why you took off?"

"I took off because we spent two days screaming at each other. Rather, I screamed, and he nodded and said, 'No, Angie. No, Angie.' I couldn't stand any more."

"Do you like your job that much?" Laura asked. "More than Tom?"

"I like to eat. I like new clothes. I want to do something besides sit around in a two-room apartment and count pennies!" Angie shouted. Then her voice broke into a half-sob. "It isn't fair. I love Tom, I really do, and I want to marry him. So why can't he be reasonable?"

Stacy shook her head. It was a side to Tom that she hadn't considered. Certainly Tom was the old-fashioned sort of male who treated women gently and would undoubtedly protect any woman, but she hadn't known his feelings ran so deeply. Nowadays, so many brides worked. Apparently Tom didn't consider that any of his affair as long as it wasn't his bride.

"Let me talk to him," Stacy said, not at all sure what she would say. But it seemed all wrong for Angie and Tom to be parted over such a minor difference after all these years of devotion.

"I don't care what you say to him as long as you don't tell him that I am here," Angie said. "I only need a few days to figure out how to get back in the house and get all my clothes, and then I'm leaving this stupid island forever."

"Oh, Angie! What about your mother?"

"She's on Tom's side. That's why I don't want to see her." Angie's lower lip jutted out. "Now, let's not mention that terrible man again. Tell me about this accident you said happened."

So Stacy explained how she had turned in the hall with the light fixture in her hand and very nearly managed to wipe out her client.

Laura cried, "He's the best-paying client we've ever had! How could you!"

"Next time I'll pick one who is behind in payments," Stacy joked, hiding her fear that she had really injured Mr. Hamilton. "Where's Priscilla?"

"Outside."

"It's getting dark. Maybe I should call her."

"All right, do that, and Angie can help me get the supper on the table," Laura said.

Stacy let herself out the kitchen door, climbed down the fire escape and called, "Here puss, puss, Priscilla. Here kitty."

The fir woods pressed in around the small, four-unit apartment building, separating it from the next building with a wall of evergreen and surrounding its other side with deep woods. Stacy wandered down the footpath, watching the dark leaves for any telltale movement. As she rounded the corner of the building, she bumped into a man.

His arms caught her before she could step back. Stacy shrieked.

"It's me, Stace."

"Tom! What on earth!"

"Angie is up at your place, isn't she? Floyd saw her get off the ferry and then later he saw her with Laura."

Stacy had to laugh. "And she thought she could keep a secret."

"I have to talk to her," Tom said.

"It won't do any good. Not tonight. She's really upset."

"Come here," Tom said, and tucked his hand under Stacy's arm. He guided her to his truck. Stacy climbed into the front seat with him. "Stacy, I am losing my mind over that girl. What kind of game is she playing?"

"I don't think she's playing a game. She really wants to marry you, you know."

"She has a funny way of showing it."

The street lights flicked on in the twilight. Stacy knew that if Angie looked out the window she would see Tom's truck. She would wonder what Stacy was doing sitting in it.

"I don't want to get mixed up in your affairs, Tom," Stacy said, "but I do think you're being a bit old-fashioned. Lots of wives work nowadays."

"Not my wife," Tom said firmly. "Listen, don't tell Angie I was here, huh? I'm glad she's back on the Island. I guess that'll have to do for now."

Should she tell him that Angie didn't plan to stay? Stacy bit her lip. She wasn't sure how involved she wanted to get. Whatever she said to either of them might be the wrong thing.

"Why don't you come back tomorrow? Or call me at the office. Only I don't know what good it will do, you're both so stubborn." She slid out of the truck and closed the door. "See you, Tom."

The spring air was filled with the smell of damp fir and the cloying sweetness of Scotch broom, an undisciplined shrub that sprung up at the edges of roads or wherever else its blowing seeds could find a sunlit spot. In the dusk she could see the luminescent piles of yellow blossoms falling over each other and the path. Wandering slowly back toward her apartment, Stacy tried to rearrange her thoughts from this Scotch broom-type jumble into some sensible order. Angie's tear-filled voice begged her not to tell Tom that she was with them, while Tom's deep mumble instructed her not to tell Angie that he knew she was with them, and between the two, she heard the tight, strained whisper of Avery Hamilton asking her to please get off him.

Perhaps the best thing to do would be drive down to some secluded beach and tell her troubles to the gulls and the night waves. She started to turn toward her car, then stopped and sighed. She could not possibly sit on a beach enjoying the sounds and smells while poor Mr. Hamilton lay in a hospital bed, possibly in terrible pain, with his leg tied up to the ceiling or whatever it was they did to broken legs. She would call the doctor and ask about Mr. Hamilton's condition. No. If the doctor were back on the Island, he would be having dinner with his family, and she would have no excuse to bother him.

She could wait until tomorrow. Or what was it Mary had said—something about taking Mr. Hamilton some books? Would he like a visitor? Somehow she didn't think so, but if he would, it was the least she could do for him. Whatever she did, she had to know that he was at least comfortable tonight. Perhaps she could phone the hospital.

As she entered the apartment, blinking her eyes in the

bright electric lights, Angie said, "So what did he want?"

"Who?"

"Tom."

"What is this? Are you two psychic?"

"No, I saw his truck out the window."

"Then why didn't you come out and talk to him?"

"Never," Angie said, her lower lip trembling. "How did he know I was here?"

"Angie, you've spent your life on this island, and you have to ask a dumb question like that? Probably about ten different people told him, which means your parents will hear soon also, so you might as well phone them. Otherwise they'll worry."

"If I go home, they'll start arguing, and I don't want to hear it. Besides, Mom won't shut the door on Tom."

"So stay here," Stacy agreed, "but at least let her know where you are." Picking up the phone book, she added, "Call her while I'm looking up the hospital number. I have to find out how poor Mr. Hamilton is."

Stacy ran her finger down the small print of the phone book until she found the right hospital number. She tried not to hear Angie, but since they were sitting less than two feet apart, tuning her out was difficult. One side of the conversation was quite enough. Apparently Angie's mother did not at all approve of Angie's behavior, and the conversation ended in some rather loud, firm statements of independence on Angie's part. She slammed down the receiver and marched into the kitchen to help Laura.

Stacy dialed the hospital, asked about Mr. Hamilton's condition, was shifted to another phone and another voice, asked her question again, heard the switchboard click, a phone ringing, and then Mr. Hamilton's voice saying, "Yes?"

She gasped in surprise, then said, "Mr. Hamilton? Is that you?"

His voice was a sleepy drawl. "Did you expect me to have expired?"

"No! I mean, I didn't expect to hear your voice, that is, I didn't want them to ring your phone, and I certainly didn't mean to disturb you, well, I *hope* I haven't woken you—"

"Miss Green," he interrupted, "why did you call?"

"Oh, I wanted to know if you were all right, but I only meant to ask the desk nurse not—"

"I can answer that. I am not well. I am not all right. Is that all you wanted to know?"

Stacy stared blankly at the phone, surprisingly at a loss for words. After a rather terrifying silence, his voice said, "Are you still there?"

"Yes," she said.

"Well, my dear, what is it you want?" He sounded like a patient uncle questioning a simple-minded child. She was half-tempted to ask him his favorite color.

Instead, she said, "I—I wondered if you would like something—anything—I mean, could I bring you some books? Or anything?"

"Come here? To the hospital?" He sounded genuinely alarmed. "That won't be necessary at all."

Stacy blurted, "I—I feel so guilty. I feel just terrible. Mr. Hamilton, you can't imagine how sorry I am. If there is anything at all that I can do for you, I wish you'd let me."

Did he laugh? She could have sworn she heard a low laugh, but then he said, "You have nothing to feel guilty about, Miss Green. I was incredibly clumsy. As I explained to the doctor, and to Miss Rouse, I slipped on the top step because I was so busy looking at the house that I wasn't watching my step. So, rest with a clear conscience and don't, uh, please don't feel obligated to come see me."

"But that isn't what happened at all!" Stacy cried. "I swung around with that damn light fixture, and it might as well have been a battering ram because—"

He cut in sharply. "You did nothing of the kind, and if you ever tell anyone you did, I will stop work on the house immediately, do you understand?" His voice softened and he said, "Now, Miss Green, there is one thing you can do for me. Kindly install that light fixture safely in the ceiling and then continue with your work on the house. I am well surrounded by people to care for me so you need not bother about that at all."

"I know you are, only I was so worried and I felt so terrible thinking of you lying there in such horrible pain, and I have spent a dreadful day worrying about you. I was afraid you'd broken your back and would be crippled forever or some other awful thing, and I would never forgive myself, honestly, because no matter what you say, it was my fault. I don't know why you don't want me to say so, but of course I will do as you ask. It's the least I can do," she rattled on, "but it honestly doesn't make me feel much better." Her voice broke in a strangled sob.

He had waited her out, letting her have her say. Now she could do nothing but sniff and fish around in her pocket for a handkerchief and wish she had never phoned the hospital. She had never felt like such a complete fool.

He said, "Stacy Green, are you crying?"

She said, "N–n–no." How terrible not to be able to say one little word without her voice breaking.

"Listen, I am not in pain. I have been given buckets of drugs and I am not only pain-free, but I am falling asleep. It was kind of you to call me. There's nothing wrong with me but a few bruises and a broken leg that is going to mend nicely, I'm sure, so don't worry about me. All right? All I really want right now is to go to sleep."

"I'm sorry," she murmured. "Please let me know if I can do anything."

He said, "Yes, definitely, *I* will call *you*." His receiver clicked down.

Stacy sat staring at the receiver in her hand as though it were a crumpled body at the foot of a staircase. Then she hung it up and wiped her eyes.

Her mind ran back over the conversation as though she were reviewing a dream. Why should he insist that she had not knocked him down the stairs? They both knew it. Tom knew it. Miss Rouse knew it. Or did they? No, Tom and Miss Rouse had been in the bedroom and would not have seen Stacy clobber Mr. Hamilton with the light fixture. Now Stacy remembered that she had explained later to Tom what had happened, after the ambulance had taken Mr. Hamilton and Miss Rouse away.

Had she mentioned to Mary that she had knocked Mr. Hamilton down the stairs? No, she didn't think so. She had told Angie and Laura the whole story when she had first arrived home, of course, but not in any great detail since Angie had been sniffing about her own problems. All right, Tom, Angie, and Laura knew she had caused the accident, which could be the same thing as telling the whole island if Tom had mentioned it to anyone since then. Still, she could not erase what had been said.

"How is he?" Laura called from the kitchen.

Stacy wandered into the small U-shaped area that formed their kitchen and said, "I don't know. I talked to him and he said he had a broken leg and bruises, and that he had taken so many drugs he couldn't feel anything."

"I expect he'll be all right," Laura said. "You, uh, you don't think he'll want to sue us or anything, do you?"

Stacy shrugged. "Apparently not."

"You don't sound very happy about that," Laura said. "Not that it matters much. We are certainly the original turnip. He can't get much blood out of us. Still, he could put us out of business. What about his hospital bills?"

"Nothing," Stacy said. "Nothing at all. He wants nothing. I don't get it. He isn't going to sue us, he doesn't want us to pay his hospital bill, and he says I should definitely complete the job."

Laura slid the broiler pan and hamburgers under the heating element, then turned back to the sink to wash her hands. "I think that's nice of him. I mean, he knows it was an accident, but a lot of people would have been furious anyway and canceled the job."

Stacy blurted, "He says it wasn't an accident! Can you imagine that! He insists he tripped, all by himself, without my help, and what is even more weird, he says that if I tell anyone that I knocked him down the stairs he will cancel the whole job. Now why is he saying that? Why is he lying? He said he even told the doctor that he tripped all by himself!"

Laura and Angie stared at her, their faces blank.

"It doesn't make any sense at all," Stacy went on. "I can't figure it out. And he so much as told me to stay away from him and not call him or come near him—"

"I can understand that," Laura interrupted, but Stacy ignored her.

"He just wants me to go on with the job and keep my mouth shut and hang that light fixture from the ceiling."

Laura laughed. "Very sensible."

"Yes, all right, joke away, girl partner, but can you honestly think of any explanation for his attitude?"

"No, not really. However, he's welcome to his attitudes, as far as I am concerned, if he can pay our bills. From this moment I am sworn to silence and will not breathe a word of the true cause of his accident. As far as I know, he tripped all by himself. What about you, Angie? Can you keep a secret?"

Angie blinked in surprise, and Stacy realized that Angie wasn't really thinking about their problem. Her thoughts had drifted in another direction. However, she had half heard the conversation, and now she said slowly, "Maybe he really did trip, Stacy. Maybe you only thought you bumped him."

"Keep that thought in your head," Laura agreed. "Now, who else have you told?"

"I told Tom," Stacy said.

"Then you better get on the phone and swear him to silence before the whole island knows the whole story."

"Don't you dare phone Tom while I'm here!" Angie shrieked.

"Don't be dumb," Laura said. "We don't have a television phone. He can't see you. Listen, go on into the bedroom while Stacy phones."

Laura had only been joking, but to her surprise,

Angie dashed out of the kitchen and ran into the bedroom and slammed the door. They both knew she was crying.

"Go ahead and phone while I get these burgers on the table, and then we can worry about Angie," Laura said.

Stacy dialed Tom's number and listened to it ring, an echo in an empty place. She waited long enough to allow him to finish with a shower, dry off, get dressed, and pick up the phone. Instead, the ringing continued without interruption. Finally, she hung up. If Tom wasn't at home, he was probably down at the local tavern talking away his troubles with friends. She could only hope that his worries about Angie would keep the story of Mr. Hamilton's fall out of his thoughts and conversation.

Returning to the kitchen she helped Laura set the table and then said, "This way, we don't know if we have a job or not. What if Tom does tell someone and it gets back to Mr. Hamilton? Will he really cancel the job?"

"Maybe you didn't hit him. Maybe, like Angie says, you only thought you did."

"I not only hit him, I fell on top of him," Stacy said. "I feel so rotten about the whole thing. Here I am wondering if he will stop the work, but honestly, that's not what I care about at all. What really worries me is if he'll be all right. What if his leg doesn't heal properly? What if he's crippled or something terrible like that?"

Laura patted her shoulder. "He'll be all right. Really. Did you ever find Priscilla?"

Stacy let out a shriek.

Laura said, "I didn't think I saw her. Okay, I'll toss you for it. Which of us goes searching in the dark for our spooky cat and which goes into the bedroom to face the tear storm?"

Neither job had much appeal, but both of them preferred to look for Priscilla. However, as Laura had been listening to Angie for several hours, Stacy agreed to tackle Angie while Laura went cat hunting.

Angie was in no mood to be consoled, having

plunged herself into another round of sobbing, but Stacy talked nonstop about anything that came into her mind, and even Angie wasn't a match for that. She dried her face and agreed to eat supper. They made it to the kitchen in time to meet Laura returning with Priscilla and almost before the burgers turned cold.

At least having Angie in the apartment provided a distraction for Stacy. Not until they had all settled down for the night, Angie on the couch and Laura and Stacy in their beds, did Stacy have time to think about her own worries. She turned over and over in her mind her conversation with Mr. Hamilton, trying to make some sense of it. Why should he insist that she lie about his accident? What difference did it make to him? Certainly he wasn't protecting his own pride by making people think he stumbled on steps all by himself.

He had said definitely that he wanted her to continue with the house, and he had said almost as definitely that he did not want her to phone him again at the hospital or come and see him.

Hours after everyone else was asleep, Stacy stared into the darkness and tried to decide what he had meant and why she was lying awake worrying about it. Many a client had given her strange instructions. None had cost her sleep before. Why should her mind refuse to leave Mr. Hamilton alone? She saw him lying on the floor, pale with pain. She saw him in the restaurant, his expression carefully controlled as he beckoned to the waiter to take care of the wine spilled on his beautiful suit. She saw the flicker of surprise in his eyes when he caught her as she tumbled from the ladder. And then she remembered the first day she met him, when she had looked up and been almost spellbound by his good looks, then irritated by his impersonal approach to decorating a house.

"Use *your* favorite color," he had said.

Why should that sentence irritate her so? What was it Tom had asked her? He had asked if she cared about Mr. Hamilton, or something close to that. She had been so wrapped up in her tears and worry about his accident that she had not paid much attention to the question.

Now it returned to haunt her. Aloud she said, "No," and her voice shocked her in the silent room. She would wake Laura.

Tom must be mad. How could Stacy possibly be interested in Mr. Hamilton? First of all, Mr. Hamilton was engaged to an absolutely breathtaking girl. Second—no first—she could not possibly be interested in a man who was carved out of marble like some Greek god, incapable of emotion. Did he ever laugh, cry, shout?

So why, she asked herself crossly, was she lying in bed in the middle of the night, wide awake, her face wet with tears at the thought of a man she did not care about?

Chapter Seven

During the next week, Mr. Hamilton's secretary phoned twice to see if Stacy had any questions and to check on the progress of the remodeling of Birch House. Yes, he'd said in answer to Stacy's queries, Mr. Hamilton was progressing nicely; he would be out of the hospital by the end of the week and into his own apartment at the hotel.

"How is his leg healing?" Stacy had asked then.

"As well as can be expected," the secretary, a Mr. Lacey, said. "I understand he will be in a wheelchair for some time. He is anxious that the remodeling project continue, Miss Green, and so if you have any problems, please contact me."

"All right," Stacy agreed, and slowly replaced the receiver. Anxious? Was Mr. Hamilton anxious? She doubted that he ever felt that much emotion about anything. As soon as that thought passed through her mind, Stacy felt a flood of guilt. The poor man was bedridden and would be in a wheelchair. He must have periods of pain, not to mention the boredom and frustration of being confined.

She thought about him lying in the hospital and wished she could do something for him, perhaps take him some puzzles or something of that sort to help him pass the time. Then she realized how empty headed that idea was. He had a raft of employees, plus Miss Rouse, to bring him anything he wanted. Apparently he talked with the secretary daily. Probably he was just as busy with his work as he would be in his office.

Stacy had made such a complete picture of him giving terse directions to employees who then hurried in all directions to do his bidding that she was genuinely surprised when, a few days later, he phoned her.

"How are you?" she asked, and then wished she could have worded the question in some more original way.

"Surviving. I wanted to know how many rooms in the downstairs of Birch House are completed."

"Oh. Well, the kitchen and bathroom are finished, and Tom has refinished the woodwork and floors in the two bedrooms, but he hasn't painted the walls. Those are the two bedrooms behind the kitchen that you thought would be useful as a servants' wing."

"Yes. All right. Do you think those bedrooms could be finished and furnished, along with the kitchen, by next Monday?"

Stacy hadn't even considered the idea. She had not yet purchased furniture for the servants' wing. However, furniture for the kitchen and the upstairs bedrooms was stored in the barn.

"Well—we could use the furniture that is supposed to go in the upstairs bedrooms, I suppose."

"Yes, do that."

"But—I mean, Mr. Hamilton, what for?"

"For me. I am planning to stay in the house for a few days. Furnish the other bedroom with twin beds. A housekeeper will use that room, and the nurse may stay one night."

"But—oh, yes—all right."

"You can manage that, can't you?" he demanded. "Or are all the workmen off fishing?"

Unconsciously Stacy's chin jutted out. "There will be no problem having the rooms ready for you by Monday," she said firmly. If she had to paint them and drag in the furniture herself, she would manage it. "However, the sound of the workmen in the rest of the downstairs will disturb you, I think. Shall I tell them to lay off while you are in residence?"

Did he laugh? She could never be sure. There was an odd choked sound, then silence. Then he said, "Fine, you arrange that. We won't be there more than three or four days, I expect. Do they have other jobs they can work at or will this cause them to lose time? If it does, I will reimburse them."

"That's not a problem," Stacy said. "They have other jobs. Mr. Hamilton, should I stock the kitchen with groceries? And what about linens? Soap? That sort of thing?"

"No, no, I have a whole hotel to draw on. Just get the rooms painted and furnished, Miss Green. I'll see you Monday."

When Stacy tried to phone Tom, she couldn't get an answer. Guessing that he was out at Birch House, she drove up Sunday Hill, spied his truck in the drive, and hurried in to find him. To her relief, he was already painting the back bedrooms. She explained what had to be done and he assured her that a Monday deadline was no problem.

"I'm sorry he is going to be in here, though," Tom said. "I've finished the sanding on all the other floors, but I had counted on staining and waxing them and finishing the rest of the painting next week. Can't do that if someone is in here, though. Too many fumes."

"Do you have any other jobs?" Stacy asked.

"This is it. I haven't taken anything else because I wanted to get out of—away from here."

"Do you still?" Stacy asked.

"Doesn't make much difference if I'm here if Angie won't see me, does it?" he said. "How is she?"

"Fine. She's working."

"How long is she planning to stay with you?"

Stacy took a deep breath, then said, "Listen, Tom, much as we like Angie, we really could use our sofa. And frankly, a sniffling girl wearing her heart on her sleeve is not exactly great company. You could help us out if you wanted to."

"How?"

"By meeting Angie halfway. There must be some point you two can agree on."

Tom's heavy jaw went hard. "As far back as I can remember, my mother had to work. Every day she came home dead tired and she still does. I won't have that with my wife."

"But it's different with Angie. She likes to work. You know how much energy she has and how she always wants to be with people. She'd go nuts stuck at home."

Tom turned away. "I know you mean well, Stace, but this is between Angie and me. Now, I'll have this paint job done tomorrow, and then I can get the furniture moved in. I'll call one of Phillips' men, and you can come out and tell us where to put stuff."

Stacy agreed, then added, "About next week. Why don't you go ahead and paint the barn?"

"I thought it was going to be torn down."

Stacy couldn't look him straight in the eye when she said, "No, I've decided it is 'authentic-old-island' and should be preserved. I'll get Phillips to get a roofer out here next week; first, you can help him and then you can do the painting."

"You're just doing that to keep me working, Stacy. It's not necessary. I can find something else. Besides, maybe Hamilton doesn't want the barn."

Now Stacy was on firmer ground. "If I tell Miss Rouse that it is an 'authentic-old-island' barn, he'll want it."

Tom laughed and chucked her under her chin with his fingertip. "Lord help the man who marries you, Stacy Green!"

"Now that you've brought up the subject, you did once say that if you hadn't already been promised to Angie, you would marry me. Is the offer still good?"

"Is the decorating business that bad?" Tom laughed.

"A promise is a promise," Stacy insisted, her dark eyes sparkling with mischief.

"Uh-uh. You're more of a career woman than Angie," Tom complained.

"That's true," Stacy admitted. "What's more, I can't cook. However, I might be willing to learn." She glanced out the window at the Scarlett hawthornes, their masses of dusty rose blossoms spilling over the back hedge, and added, "I'd even learn to sew and wash windows to live in a dream house like this."

"It's a real honeymoon house, isn't it?" Tom agreed.

A honeymoon house? Stacy had not thought of it that

way. Now she saw that he was right. With its romantic old woodwork and its cottage garden and picket fence, Birch House looked like something out of a picture book. In her imagination she could see a bride and groom—he was in traditional tux and she was in white satin—strolling hand in hand up the front steps. They turned, kissed, drew apart, and their perfect profiles were outlined against the front door.

Then the perfect profiles were topped by glowing crowns of hair—his red, hers silver—and Stacy had to shake her head to clear away the mental image of an Art Deco painting of Dominic Rouse and Avery Hamilton.

Tom finished painting and papering the two first-floor bedrooms on Saturday. Sunday, Stacy played traffic cop, directing Tom and a couple of his friends as they carried in the furniture from the barn. By the time the rooms were arranged, it was midafternoon and, although Tom offered to stay longer, Stacy told him to leave. She knew the three of them were anxious to push their fishing boat out on the high tide.

"Fish don't bite in midafternoon," Tom assured her.

"No, but by the time you collect all your gear and pick up bait, and probably stop for lunch and beer, it won't be afternoon."

Tom rapped her lightly on the top of her head with his knuckles. "Yes, mother."

Stacy made a face at him. "Shoo. All of you. I need privacy. I can't think with you three apes tromping around."

"I know. You want to rearrange a few chairs, hang some ornaments, and probably put your back out of whack moving the bureau."

"How did you know?" Stacy demanded.

"You have that look in your eye. I've seen it before."

"I won't move anything heavy," Stacy promised. "But I do have some quilts to dig out and some candlesticks and things to set around."

When they were gone, Stacy wandered, deep in thought, through the bedrooms and the kitchen. The polished floors shone at the edges of the old Oriental rugs. The old pieces of furniture that she had so carefully selected fit into the rooms as though the rooms had been designed to fit them. For a moment Stacy felt transported back to the turn of the century, as if she were the original owner of the house. With all the floors and walls newly waxed, painted, or papered, and the furniture pieces either refinished or newly cleaned and waxed, it was like stepping into a room in another time.

Stacy spread an old linen tablecloth with embroidered edges on the round oak table in the kitchen and then pushed in the high-backed chairs. Above the tile stove she hung a collection of kitchen gadgets. On its top she placed a copper teakettle, its color mellowed with age and a thousand polishings.

During her scouting trips through old houses and antique shops she had uncovered a marvelous collection of linen dresser scarves. These had been carefully mended and laundered by an Island seamstress. Stacy arranged them in the bedrooms, then topped them with a few ornaments that included a china dresser set decorated in an old Dutch village pattern. She knew that the housekeeper would make up the beds, but rather than leave the new mattresses, ordered to fit the old brass bedsteads, uncovered, she smoothed over each of them an exquisite handmade quilt, true collector's items —just the sort of touch cherished by *Homes of Distinction.*

She opened the windows a few inches to let in the air, and it filled the rooms with the scent of lilac. Stacy flipped a few of the light switches to be sure Tom had put bulbs in the fixtures, then let herself out the kitchen door and locked it. This was the first time she had locked Birch House and she supposed it really didn't need to be locked, but now that some of the furnishings were inside she thought perhaps she should. Robberies seldom occurred on the Island, but recently several summer homes had been stripped of antiques, probably by professional thieves. As Birch House could not be seen from any other house, it could be a target.

Walking down the drive to her car, Stacy had a sudden thought. Had Mr. Hamilton wanted a phone installed? He hadn't mentioned it. Perhaps he assumed she would do that. He hadn't mentioned water and electricity either, but of course both were connected. Oh, dear. Why hadn't she thought to ask him about the phone? It took at least a week to get a phone installed and that would do him no good at all.

The next morning, when Stacy's desk phone rang in her office, she was still wondering about the phone problem and had not thought of a more immediate problem.

"Miss Green? Mr. Lacey here." His voice could have frozen a volcano. "I am phoning from a house down the hill from Birch House. Mr. Hamilton and the housekeeper and nurse and a delivery man are waiting on the front steps of Birch House. For some reason the doors are locked and we do not have keys."

"Oh, my goodness," Stacy squeaked. "Well—uh—the key, I mean, I have them here. Wait right there, Mr. Lacey. I'll be right out."

"I will wait for you at Birch House," Mr. Lacey said.

When Stacy drove up Sunday Hill and parked across the drive from the house, she saw the nurse and housekeeper, both uniformed, standing as rigid as toy soldiers on the front step. A man in work overalls lounged against the side of a delivery truck. A man in the most conservative dark gray suit that Stacy had ever seen stood stiffly by the limousine pulled in behind the truck in the driveway.

The only person who did not seem to be waiting for her was Mr. Hamilton. He sat in a wheelchair at the edge of the brick walkway, his back to the others, gazing out toward the water.

"I am so sorry," Stacy said, before she was even out of her car, and she continued apologizing all the way up the drive to the front door. "Until the new hardware was put in the doors, I didn't have any keys to give you, and after Mr. Phillips gave me the keys, the ones I have now for the new locks, I never thought about giving them to you because, of course, I knew you had the keys to the original locks from the realtor, and so somehow I forgot that you wouldn't—"

The man in the dark suit, who was obviously Mr.

Lacey, interrupted. "Miss Green, would you please open the door?"

Stacy fumbled with the key, dropped it twice, bent to retrieve it, finally managed to fit it into the lock, and opened the door. "Can I help you bring things in?" she asked.

Mr. Lacey said, "No, thank you," in a tone that clearly dismissed her.

He and the housekeeper and the nurse and the delivery man, carrying in luggage and boxes, brushed past her as though she weren't there.

Behind her, Mr. Hamilton said, "Good morning, Miss Green."

"Oh, Mr. Hamilton!" Stacy swung around. He still had his back to the house and to her. She hurried across the path to greet him. "I am so sorry you had to wait."

"Why?" He glanced up at her and she thought he looked, for a brief moment, as though he had been laughing. "The view is pleasant and the day is warm and I am not going anywhere."

Stacy looked down at his leg, which was encased in a cast, and said, "No, I suppose not. Mr. Hamilton, I forgot to ask if you wanted to have a phone installed? Now it is really too late because the phone company always takes at least a week to come out, so by the time they installed it, you would be leaving, and so I should have thought—"

"You're rattling again, Miss Green."

"What? I'm what?"

"Saying the same thing over and over."

"Oh! Oh, I am sorry, it's only that, you see—"

"You're doing it again," he interrupted. "Miss Green, my secretary will be appalled to learn that there is no phone as he is returning to Seattle in an hour and had planned to remain there while staying in constant contact with me by phone. He has done that ever since I have been imprisoned in this cast and unable to escape him."

"Oh, Mr. Hamilton, I am so sorry—"

"Don't apologize. I am delighted. This may be the most peaceful three days I've spent in ages."

"But if Mr. Lacey is going back to Seattle, what will you do for a car? I mean, I know you can't drive, but won't your housekeeper need to get to the stores?"

"I fervently hope so," he said flatly. "Mr. Lacey will return in the delivery truck, we will keep the car, and if I can manage it, the housekeeper and the nurse will spend as much time shopping as possible. With any luck, they will lose their way to town often and spend hours finding their way back."

Stacy laughed. "Are you that desperate for solitude?"

"You've no idea. Never before have I been flat on my back at the mercy of my staff, family, fiancée, and heaven knows who else."

"I feel awfully guilty about that," Stacy began.

He cut her short. "If you apologize to me one more time about anything at all, I shall fire you."

Surely he was joking. How could he say such things with a straight face? Stacy peered at him and he looked her right in the eyes. For some odd reason that she preferred not to think about, she had a lurching feeling in her heart. Or was it her stomach? She had forgotten what a soft, quiet gray his eyes were.

She started to say that she was sorry, bit the words back just in time and said, "Yes, all right."

"That's better."

The nurse joined them and said, "Mr. Hamilton, would you like to go inside now?"

"No," he said. "I will stay out here for a while. Miss Bills, this is Miss Green, the decorator."

Miss Bills smiled and said that she knew who Miss Green was and, all at once, Stacy felt quite sure that Miss Bills, Mr. Lacey, and the housekeeper had had a lengthy discussion about that decorator who had changed the hardware on the doors without delivering the keys to the owner. The whole conversation could have been written on Miss Bills's forehead—that was how clearly it showed. Miss Bills was a thin, tall woman, rather strong looking, with a pinched face and a voice that was accustomed to giving commands.

After Mr. Lacey drove off with the truck, Mr. Hamilton suggested to Miss Bills that she go to town with the housekeeper, Mrs. Enderby, to check out the stores and buy supplies.

"I have everything I need," Miss Bills said.

"Yes, of course, but Mrs. Enderby may need help."

"I wouldn't want to leave you alone, Mr. Hamilton."

"Miss Green will stay until you return." His tone left no room for argument, from either Stacy or Miss Bills, and Stacy realized that the one person who was even more accustomed to giving orders than Miss Bills was Mr. Hamilton. Miss Bills nodded but her disapproval showed clearly on her face. She turned and marched into the house, head high, back stiff.

"My loving fiancée found that nurse for me," Mr. Hamilton said. "I am determined to tolerate her for twenty-four hours and then back to Seattle she goes."

"Why twenty-four hours?"

"I pride myself in being able to get along with anyone, Miss Green, and I don't like to lose my self-esteem over one temporary employee. However, the farther I can keep her from me during the twenty-four hours, the greater my chance of success, don't you think?"

Stacy said, "I am sure she is a very good nurse." If the nurse had been handpicked by Miss Rouse, Stacy did not want to be in the middle of a quarrel.

"I thought you would be on my side," said Mr. Hamilton.

"Against whom?"

"Miss Bills, of course. What did you think?"

Stacy decided that she would rather not say what she thought. Instead, she said, "I could give them the wrong directions to town so that they would be gone longer, if you like."

"I knew you were clever, but I underestimated you," he said. "You are also a lady with a truly kind heart."

Stacy laughed. When the nurse and housekeeper emerged from the house together, Mr. Hamilton said, "Mrs. Enderby, are you sure you know the way to town?"

Mrs. Enderby nodded, and Miss Bills said clearly, "I am sure *I* do," so that was that. Stacy could not really have lied to them, she knew, or at least she didn't think she could, and she was relieved that she did not need to act on her suggestion. She had really meant it as a joke.

Then, to her surprise, after the car backed out of the driveway, Mrs. Enderby turned up Sunday Hill instead of down.

"They *are* going the wrong way!" she exclaimed.

"Where will that direction take them?"

"To the north end of the Island. Eventually they will circle back to town, but they'll have added seven or eight miles to their trip."

"Maybe more if they choose the wrong turns."

"Oh, dear, that's right. All the crossings look the same, really, just lots of fir trees."

"Delightful. I could have half a day's peace."

Looking down at him, Stacy realized that Mr. Hamilton looked weary and a bit pale. Remembering not to apologize, she said, "I could go inside and do a few things and leave you here alone, if you'd like. But I wouldn't be far, so if you needed anything you could call. Or perhaps I could bring a bell out for you, or a pan and spoon if I can't find a bell, and come to think of it—"

"A pan and spoon?" he asked. "What for?"

"To bang on so that I could hear you," Stacy explained.

"Stacy Green, I love the way your mind works," he said slowly, and he gazed at her so intently that Stacy turned away. "I am quite all right here by myself," he said after a moment's silence. "If you have something to do, go ahead. You'd be surprised how loud I can shout if I need you."

"It isn't that I have anything to do. Well, yes, I do, of course, if you're all right alone. I do need to re-check a couple of measurements, but it's not important. I just don't want to be in your way if you would like to, well maybe you would like a nap?"

"I have never taken a nap that I can remember, except when I have closed my eyes and pretended to be asleep to avoid Miss Bills, and I really can't imagine how I could take a nap sitting up, so unless you are planning to take me inside and tuck me in bed, I presume I will remain awake. Oh, my Lord!" A look of surprise widened his eyes.

"What's wrong? Are you in pain? Can I get you some aspirin or something?" Stacy blurted.

"Listen to me!" he exclaimed. "I am rattling."

"You're what?"

"I am rattling. Like you, Miss Green. I am talking on and on like you do, repeating ideas and explaining things that don't need to be explained."

"Well, I never!" Stacy said, outraged.

He laughed and said, "Yes, you do, all the time."

"Mr. Hamilton, I am going inside and I shall leave you by yourself so that you can enjoy the total silence of your surroundings in total peace without me rattling around, and if you desperately need anything you may shout, and I may hear you or I may not." Stacy swung toward the house and intended to do exactly what she had said, but he caught her wrist in his large hand.

"Please don't," he said. Was he apologizing? Not exactly, but Stacy guessed that was about as close as he would come to an apology. "I am bored with the deadly people who surround me, Miss Green, but I am also bored with myself. I would like you to talk to me. Listen, I know there's a deck of cards somewhere in the house, because Nurse Bills tried a dozen times to convince me that I should play cards with her, so why not find them and bring them out? Do you play gin rummy?"

An impish gleam crept into Stacy's dark eyes. "A little," she said lightly. He released her wrist and she hurried into the house to find the cards. When she came out, she found that Mr. Hamilton had wheeled his chair over to one of the benches at the edge of the path. He glanced at the cards in her hand and smiled.

"You were right," Stacy explained. "They were on your bedside table."

"What exciting bedtimes I have to look forward to," he said in a flat tone.

Stacy sat on the end of the bench and spread the cards out in front of her. While he shuffled and dealt, she stared at the firm, quick movements of his hands. Remembering the warmth of his hand on her wrist, she looked away.

"Strangely quiet," he said.

"I don't know what to say. I can't apologize or you'll fire me, and I can't rattle or you'll laugh at me."

"Have I intimidated you that much, Miss Green?"

If he meant that as a joke, he wasn't getting away with it. "Yes," Stacy said firmly.

"All right, I probably have. Now I wish I hadn't. Go ahead and rattle."

Stacy pressed her lips together and picked up her cards. She stared at them for a moment, played her hand, and after no more than two minutes, spread her cards on the bench and said, "Gin."

He glared at her. He now realized that her silence was a declaration of war. What he didn't know was that Stacy had been an avid card player for years and could beat almost anyone at gin rummy.

After forty-five minutes in almost total silence and a string of defeats, Mr. Hamilton threw down his cards. Staring at Stacy, he said, "I don't suppose you'd like to try arm wrestling instead?"

She broke her mask of concentration and laughed. "No, I think you could win that game."

He sat back, let his eyes roam over her face, then said slowly, "I know you have talent and taste, my dear Miss Green, but in the months that I have been dealing with you I have wondered how you managed to run a business. I rather thought your partner must do the management part. Now I think I was wrong. You only look like a flutterbrain. And act like one. And talk like one. But you don't think like one, do you? You are quite capable of concentrating your mind."

Stacy shrugged. "I never said I wasn't."

"And you are still a bit angry with me."

"No, I—why should I be?" she said, surprised.

"I can think of many reasons but I have no idea which one is yours. I only know that so much silence from you must stem from some sort of annoyance."

"Oh, that." Stacy bit her lip, wondered what to say,

then blurted, "To tell the truth, I am not sure what to say to you because what I really want to say is how terrible it makes me feel to see you stuck there in that wheelchair; I can see from your face that you've been in pain—you look very tired and run down—and it shocks me. I want to do something to make up to you; there must be something I could do, but no, you won't even let me apologize or even, for that matter, take the blame for your accident—"

"No, I won't," he interrupted.

"Well, I can't see why! We both know perfectly well that I did knock you down the stairs with that fool ceiling fixture—"

"Did you get that installed?"

"Yes, of course, and as I was saying—"

"I was trying to stop you from saying. I was trying to tactfully change the subject, but I am not very good at tact."

"Mr. Hamilton!" Stacy cried in exasperation, "you say you want me to talk to you and then you make all sorts of rules and cut me off whenever I start on a subject you don't like. . . . Then you pretend that things aren't the way they are—oh honestly!—I don't know what to say!"

He leaned forward and said softly, "Listen, missy, you're right, of course, and giving you instructions without explanations is impossible, I see. It has always been impossible since the first time I walked in your office, and I should remember that by now. All right, I will explain, and then please let's talk about something else.

"First, about my fall down the stairs. My dear, you couldn't have done a better job if you'd hit me with an Army tank. I know it and you know it, but we both also know that you didn't mean to knock me down the stairs." He paused, then asked, "Did you?"

"Of course not!"

"All right. So that's that. No matter who takes the blame, it will take my leg exactly the same amount of time to heal. And no matter who takes the blame, it will be my business that will pay all the hospital bills and absorb the costs, since I don't imagine you're in any position to pay. However, if you take the blame my lawyers are going to get all excited about the question of responsibility; I shall have to override them and go through bothersome arguments, right? So if you let me say I fell down the stairs, you will save me needless discussions."

Stacy opened her mouth but couldn't think of what to say. Then, after a minute of staring at him stupidly, she stammered, "That—that is very kind of you."

"Certainly it is," he said firmly. Then he added, "Well, not really. I am not as worried about my lawyers as all that. They take my instructions. But my fiancée is another small problem. First, if she knew you caused my fall, she would want you, uh, removed from the job."

"I don't blame her," Stacy said. "I should think she would and I should think you would, too."

"What for? My leg is broken. Firing you won't mend it. I hired you to decorate my house and I like your work, so firing you now wouldn't really benefit me, would it? However, I tend to think more objectively than Dominic. Sometimes she is a bit emotional."

"Well, she is supposed to be emotional about things that concern you," Stacy exclaimed. "After all, she loves you. It must be terrible for her to see you suffering."

To her surprise, he laughed. "Miss Green, you have caused me far more suffering with your gin rummy than I have had from my broken leg, and I don't see you feeling terrible about that."

"That's different," Stacy said firmly. "Do you want to play some more?"

He shook his head and she thought he looked tired. Then he said, "Why don't you check the kitchen and see if the housekeeper brought some coffee with her? They brought boxes of stuff from the hotel. Surely someone thought of coffee."

Stacy put the cards back in their box and started for the house, then turned back to be sure he was comfortable before she left him for any length of time. Perhaps she should bring out a quilt to wrap around his legs. A light breeze ruffled the new leaves of the birches, and the spring sunlight cast dappled patterns across his dark red hair.

When she asked about the quilt, he said, "No, I'm fine, really. I'll just wheel my chair out from under these trees into the sun." He glanced up at the birches, and the light smoothed the lines from his face and sparkled in his eyes. He looked like a teenager.

Stacy hurried back to him, caught the handles of the chair, and said, "I'll move you, Mr. Hamilton. You just relax."

But as she turned the chair it swung around much more quickly than she had expected. The arm of the chair banged against her leg, and her ankle twisted on the edge of the walkway. Mr. Hamilton moved quickly to steady her, and somehow—Stacy never quite understood how—she ended up falling across him. His strong hands caught her, steadied her, then settled her on his lap. Stacy stared wide eyed, too embarrassed to think or move or speak, her mouth half-open like an idiot's. She simply could not force herself to believe that she had managed to topple over him a third time.

While she stared into his face, shocked, his hands slid slowly up her arms until he cradled her face between his palms. There was nothing, no expression, on his face to tell her what he was thinking, and all Stacy could think was that she had been right the first time—he really was the handsomest man she had ever seen. When he kissed her, Stacy stopped thinking at all. His mouth was warm and firm, and a kind of sunlit joy flooded her.

Then she remembered who she was and where she was. The only thing Stacy could not remember was why she was kissing this man and why she felt so comfortable and happy about it. She pushed herself away from him, almost falling from his lap as she stumbled to her feet. Then she stood staring down at him, frozen. She expected him to laugh or make some joking remark. He gazed back at her, and she had no more idea what he was thinking now than she ever had.

"I—oh, I—must be going," Stacy mumbled, bumping into a tree trunk as she backed away from him. She turned and hurried to her car, finding that by some miracle her keys were still in the ignition. She concentrated on starting the car and backing it out of the driveway, not daring to look toward Mr. Hamilton. If he had called to her, she would have heard him, but he didn't.

It wasn't until she reached the bottom of Sunday Hill that Stacy remembered that she had promised to stay with him until the nurse returned. She pulled her car off to the side of the road and stopped. Sitting behind the wheel with her fingers frozen around it, Stacy shivered violently in the warm day. What should she do? She couldn't go back and face him. How could she? What could she possibly say to him? Was he as embarrassed as she was? She hadn't meant to fall in his lap. Probably he hadn't meant to kiss her. Unfortunately, it hadn't been a light brotherly kiss, the kind of kiss Tom might give her if she stumbled into his lap. Not like that at all.

"I am a grown woman," Stacy muttered to herself. "A kiss isn't that big a deal. It is not as though it meant anything."

She could say that to herself but she couldn't convince herself. Unfortunately, she knew his kiss did mean something, at least to her. He had held her too long. His hands had moved from her face and slid around her back until his arms circled her. He had kissed her as though—but she couldn't think what it had been like. His kiss had been warm and wonderful and, for a moment, very exciting. Yes. He had kissed her as though they were lovers, as though they meant something to each other. And the trouble was that, although she felt sure she meant nothing to him, she was equally sure that he meant a great deal to her.

Tom was right. She was in love with Mr. Avery Hamilton. She could not possibly drive back to Birch House and act nonchalant. She would stammer and make a fool of herself. He would see in her face the way it was with her. And yet she couldn't leave him alone. What if he tried to turn his chair around, and it tipped over? What if a strange dog ran into the yard? What if, what if, oh, she didn't know what. But she did know that she had a responsibility. Slowly, she backed her car onto the road, turned down a side road, and drove up the other side of Sunday Hill. She left her car at the edge of the narrow gravel road, climbed a fence, wandered through a small apple orchard, and crossed a meadow. Finally she came out near a stand of firs at the top of the hill. From there, just as she had thought, she was able to see down into the yard of Birch House. As a child she had explored every hill of the Island, and although her wandering days were several years behind her, she still remembered most of the paths and viewpoints.

He was sitting in his wheelchair, staring out across the hillside toward the Sound. If he raised his head, he would be able to see her. She stepped back into the shadow of the trees. He did not raise his head. He sat so quietly that she thought he might be asleep. Then she remembered that he could not sleep sitting up. He had wanted a cup of coffee. Was he cold? Was he uncomfortable? Stacy felt guilty and torn and miserable.

While she tried to decide what to do, a car turned into the drive of Birch House. When she saw that it was the housekeeper and the nurse, she turned away and went back to her own car. At least she wouldn't have to worry about his comfort now.

Chapter Eight

The next morning Stacy worked through a stack of paper on her desk, some of her thoughts on the work, the rest tumbling over all that had happened. She had sent Laura out to Birch House to see if Mr. Hamilton had any objections to having Tom work on the barn that week. It was cowardly, she would be the first to admit it, but she was not ready to face Mr. Hamilton this morning. Not after yesterday. Not after last night.

As though the whole embarrassing episode of the previous day had not been enough, she had spent a wretched evening listening to Angie tearfully pouring out her heart. Unfortunately, Laura had not been there to help; she had gone to dinner in Seattle with some friends.

"It was rotten, rotten, rotten of you to desert me," Stacy had told her the next day, as soon as they were out of the apartment and Angie's hearing.

"Sorry, dearie, but how could I know Angie would fall apart again?"

"Because she falls apart every night. Still, I don't suppose there is much point in both of us suffering. I do wish I could get her to at least talk to Tom. And vice versa. They are both so stubborn."

Laura said, "Thank heaven Angie's run out of vacation time. She'll have to go back to work tomorrow. I think she'll be better if she has something to do, don't you? It's not good for her to sit around in our apartment all day, brooding about Tom."

"She'll be better unless Tom walks into the bank where she works," Stacy said.

"Don't even think about that," Laura said.

It was then that Stacy had said, very casually she hoped, "By the way, I have tons of papers to get through here. I wonder if you could do me a little favor? Tom wants to work on the barn up at Birch House this week, but I forgot to ask Mr. Hamilton if that would be a bother for them. Would you mind stopping by?"

"Fine," Laura said. "I'd like to take a look at that job, anyway." Then she added mischievously, "And I wouldn't mind seeing the handsome Mr. Hamilton again, either."

Stacy didn't reply. Keeping her problems to herself was the only thing she could do, under the circumstances. It was bad enough that Tom had seen through her feelings about Mr. Hamilton before she herself had even known about them. She could not bear to tell Laura about yesterday. She could hardly bear to think about it to herself.

And so when Laura breezed in just before noon, the news she brought from Birch House did nothing to ease Stacy's discomfort.

"I saw our dear Mr. Hamilton," Laura said, "and he wouldn't mind a bit if Tom works on the barn. I got the definite feeling that Mr. Hamilton would be relieved, even pleased, to have a man around to defend him from the housekeeper and the nurse. When I arrived, they were both fussing over him as though he were the emperor on his deathbed. Now then, I also have a message for you. He wants you to come up this afternoon as he has something to discuss with you, and he said that, no, he could not send a message, he must see you in person."

Stacy's heart sank. "Did he say why?"

"No. He didn't say and he didn't act as though he thought I could take care of the problem, whatever it was, and you know, Stacy love, I am not one to pester or annoy a rich client by questioning his requests."

"No, of course not. I'll go out after lunch." For a quick moment Stacy thought of resigning from the job. But she knew that she could not do that. It would mean more than a loss of income for her. It would mean putting Laura and Tom back on poverty street. No matter what her personal feelings were, she owed both of them the income and prestige that would be gained from this job. It would mean many future jobs for all of them, especially if Birch House really was to be featured in *Homes of Distinction.*

After lunch Stacy drove up Sunday Hill and parked in the drive. To her dismay she noticed that besides the housekeeper's car, another equally expensive automobile blocked the drive. Was fussy Mr. Lacey inside? On the other hand, if he were, any conversation between herself and Mr. Hamilton would be kept formal and at a minimum, so perhaps that was just as well.

When the housekeeper answered Stacy's knock, she said, "They're around on the side patio, Miss Green."

"Thanks, I'll walk around outside," Stacy said. She turned back down the front steps and across the front garden. When she turned the corner of the house, the first thing she saw was Mr. Hamilton, seated on the octagonal bench beneath the cherry tree. A pair of crutches leaned against the bench. He looked up and smiled.

Then a movement near the house caught the edge of Stacy's glance, and she turned and saw Dominic Rouse standing in front of the new French doors that led to the living room. Her face assumed a frozen smile just as Stacy turned, and Stacy knew at once that she had walked into an argument. She could feel the tension as though it were a sharp wind. Yet, overhead, the sun shone brightly and cast its patterns through the blossoms and across the gravel patio.

"Good afternoon, Miss Green," Miss Rouse said.

"Good—hello, how nice to see you," Stacy murmured. She turned to Mr. Hamilton and added, "It's nice to see you, too, I mean, nice to see you out of the wheelchair."

Mr. Hamilton said solemnly, "Wheelchairs can be quite dangerous. I feel safer on crutches."

"That's ridiculous," Dominic said, her voice controlled but a bit tight and a tone too high. "You aren't at all able to take care of yourself on crutches. You should be at the hotel where you'd have a proper staff to look after you. Don't you think so, Miss Green?"

"Well, I—uh—" Stacy hesitated. She had no idea what to say.

Mr. Hamilton saved her the bother. "Miss Green knows that I am quite capable of taking care of myself. She also knows that wheelchairs can cause terrible accidents. I hardly think it fair to ask her about that, however."

How could he say that? Stacy thought she would die on the spot. If he wasn't embarrassed by yesterday's accident, she certainly was, and she felt like turning and running. However, she forced herself to remember that any foolish move would only make things worse.

"What are you talking about?" Miss Rouse asked.

Mr. Hamilton said, "I'm really trying to change the subject, dear." Was there a malicious twinkle in his eye? It was hard to tell with him because his face was so controlled, but Stacy thought so. She looked away and stared up at the cherry tree branches.

He added, "I don't think we should drag Miss Green into our disagreements, Dominic."

"Why not? Are you afraid she'll agree with me? Any sensible person would." Swinging toward Stacy, Miss Rouse smiled her sweetest smile and said, "Miss Green, you tell him. It is insane for him to stay here in this damp climate when he could be in Florida or Spain or Italy recuperating on a warm beach. Isn't that right?"

Stacy's eyes widened. "Could he?"

"That's what I think he should do. We could be on our way in three or four days, or even less. I have to go home by way of New York, of course; there are so many plans to change with this dreadful broken leg thing, but his nurse could take him anywhere, and I would join him, and it would be ever so much more sensible."

"I am perfectly comfortable right here," Mr. Hamilton said.

"Avery, you're being stubborn. You're miles from anywhere here, and I have to go back to New York, you know I do, and I don't want to fly all the way back here again. By the time I get back you'll be thoroughly bored and ready to leave this place, and then I'll have to get right back on a plane, and, oh honestly, can't you be sensible?"

"I am being sensible. I am comfortable here and here I stay."

Miss Rouse shrugged but was careful not to frown. "I suppose I could do most of the plan-changing over the phone, but it would be very difficult, and besides, there are people I should see in person."

"Why change anything?" Mr. Hamilton asked.

"Avery! You can't walk down an aisle on crutches! It would ruin everything!"

Down the aisle on crutches? Stacy's brain whirled. Why hadn't she thought of that? No wonder Mr. Hamilton had said that he didn't want Miss Rouse to know how the accident had occurred. No wonder he was so sure Miss Rouse would insist on firing her if she knew Stacy had knocked Mr. Hamilton downstairs. Stacy hadn't just broken his leg, she had thoroughly inconvenienced their wedding plans.

"Are you postponing your wedding?" Stacy blurted.

Miss Rouse said, "What else can we do? Avery can't go down the aisle in a wheelchair or on crutches, can he?"

"Yes, I can," he said firmly.

"No, you can't. It would look terrible! Now, Avery, you know I haven't complained about postponing the wedding or said a word about the trouble it will cause, you know I haven't. You didn't break your leg on purpose and I'm not blaming you, darling, but after all, I'm the one who has to change all the plans and do all the rushing around. I do think you could at least go back East with me so that I won't have to come back out here for you; then we could take the nurse and go on to some place warm." Turning gracefully toward Stacy with that smooth, grand lady movement that seemed so natural for Dominic Rouse, she asked, "Does it ever get really warm here?"

"Not like Florida, no," Stacy said. "Of course, I grew

up in this climate and so I like it. Miss Rouse, I feel terrible that you have to postpone your wedding."

Dominic smiled too sweetly, as though Stacy were a scullery maid who needed to be talked to as one might talk to a child. "That's kind of you, dear. It's my own fault, of course. If I hadn't insisted on buying this place, Avery wouldn't have fallen down those stupid old stairs. I take full blame for it, but what I cannot understand is why he now wants to stay in this house instead of coming home to New York."

"I will be back in New York in time for the original date of our wedding," he said. His voice had that flat, inflexible tone that probably closed board meetings.

Miss Rouse's veneer cracked. "Avery, stop that! You *know* we have to postpone the wedding and I won't argue about it anymore. Just ask anyone! Ask Miss Green!" To Stacy she demanded, "Miss Green, if your fiancé couldn't walk down the aisle on his own two feet, wouldn't you want to postpone the wedding?"

"I—I don't know. I mean, I haven't ever even thought about getting married—I—I don't know—" Stacy knew she would rattle around unable to answer and unable to stop trying to answer.

Fortunately, Mr. Hamilton cut in, "This is between you and me, Dominic. Now why don't you go on back to New York and cancel the wedding, and when I feel up to it, I'll join you. I don't want to argue this anymore. I don't want to make any other plans. If the leg takes longer to heal than expected—and you know the doctor said it might—I don't want to go through a whole different change of plans."

"But this is absurd! If you're here and I'm in New York, I can't even talk to you! You don't even have a phone in this godforsaken place!" Her voice rose to a shriek.

He said quietly, "You are the one who wanted a house in this godforsaken place, if that is how you choose to describe it."

Dominic's face tightened until her eyes were slits and her mouth was rigid with anger. She turned on Stacy, saying, "Why didn't you have a phone installed?

Don't you think it's dangerous for Mr. Hamilton to be here without a phone? He can't even call a doctor. You people are so provincial! Can't you do anything right?"

"I—I—yes, I should have, only nothing was said—I am truly sorry, Miss Rouse, I—"

"Stop apologizing," Mr. Hamilton commanded. "Dominic, if I had wanted a phone, I would have told Mr. Lacey to order it. I am perfectly happy without a phone. Now if you're going back to New York, you can do me a favor on the way. Take Miss Bills and lose her somewhere."

"Miss Bills! Avery, I personally picked her because she is very well qualified to look after you, and you cannot possibly stay here without a nurse! I never heard of anything so absurd."

If she weren't there, Stacy wondered, would they be even angrier with each other? Or would they suddenly stop shouting and kiss and make up the way her parents used to do? Stacy glanced around, desperately trying to think of what she might do to excuse herself and leave them.

Before she could think of anything, Mr. Hamilton said, "Miss Green, your partner was here this morning and mentioned something about this Tom person coming back to work tomorrow. I think that would be fine, and I wonder if I could also hire him to do a few errands for me and help me if I need help?"

Stacy said, "You wouldn't need to hire Tom. He appreciates the job you've given him. He'd be happy to do anything to help you."

"Isn't Tom the painter?" Miss Rouse demanded. "Surely you don't think a painter can substitute for a nurse?"

"Surely you don't think I am going to let Miss Bills lift me in and out of a bathtub," Mr. Hamilton shot back.

Stacy turned away to hide the grin that she could not control. She hadn't understood why Mr. Hamilton needed Tom's help, but when he put it so bluntly she couldn't help smiling. She knew that big, good-natured

Tom wouldn't mind helping at all, but he would do it as a favor, not for pay.

"You are impossible," Miss Rouse exploded. "You really are, Avery! I can see you've made your mind up and I am not going to stand here arguing with you. I think I will go on back to New York tonight and do all the necessary rearranging by myself. Then I will come back out here as soon as I can. And I will tell Mr. Lacey to order the phone installation."

"Do whatever you like but take Miss Bills!"

Miss Rouse clutched her hands until her knuckles shone white. Turning, she marched into the house. Stacy could hear her high heels clicking across the bare floors. Unable to look at Mr. Hamilton, she stared at the open French doors. A few minutes later she saw Miss Bills, purse in hand, hurrying across the front hall on the far side of the unfinished living room. The front door slammed. The car started. Finally she heard it back up, turn, and rush down Sunday Hill. In a moment, it was out of earshot.

Because she could think of nothing else to say, Stacy said weakly, "I hope you won't fire the housekeeper, too. Tom can't cook."

Mr. Hamilton's laugh surprised her. "And what about you?"

"I can't either, at least not anything I would want to serve to anyone else."

"I am a gourmet cook," he said flatly. "Someday I will have to teach you."

"You are?"

"Close your mouth, Miss Green. It is hanging open. My dear, I have many talents. Cooking is an easy hobby to take along for someone who lives on airplanes and in apartments."

"Yes, I suppose so."

"If I stay here long enough in this house, I might take up gardening."

"Not with your leg in a cast. Mr. Hamilton, you can't imagine how terrible I feel that your wedding plans are changed. It's all my—"

"Don't you dare say it," he cut in.

"Well, I am, just the same."

"All right. You can repay me with a favor."

"Yes?"

"Do you know the people who hook up phones on the Island?"

"Sure, of course. I'll do what I can to hurry them up, but I must warn you that even with me pestering I can't—"

"Indeed, don't. What I would like you to do is tell them that I am in no hurry; in fact, if they don't get out here for a month or two months, that will be fine."

"A month? You're planning to stay here a month?"

He shrugged. "I don't really know. But I do know that I don't want a phone installed in this house. It will ring constantly and what I really want now is some peace. Lacey can get himself over here for a couple of hours every day and then he can leave. If I have a phone, he'll be calling me around the clock."

"Perhaps Miss Rouse won't be gone too long."

He shrugged at that. "What I need is someone to talk to who won't bring me problems or arguments. Do you think you can manage to stop by occasionally with those books, magazines, and other whatevers that you mentioned when I was in the hospital?"

"Oh. Yes, yes, of course, Mr. Hamilton. I'd be coming by every day, anyway, to see how Tom is coming along with the barn, so it isn't any bother at all, really, so if you think of anything else you want—" Stacy stopped abruptly. A picture of herself in his lap flashed through her mind. For a moment she had forgotten. Had he?

No, he hadn't. She knew that when he said, "You could beat me at gin rummy, though I think a truly kind person would let an invalid win once in a while. It should be safe enough now that I am out of that wheelchair."

Stacy froze her face into a mask of businesslike efficiency. It took considerable effort. It also required that she not look into his eyes. If she did, she might melt down to nothing at his feet, or worse yet, she might blush. Blushing wasn't a thing she did easily or often, but she had a feeling that she might start being a blusher any moment. She stared hard at a point just above his eyebrows.

"Mr. Hamilton, I don't know how much free time I will have, but I will be glad to run errands for you, and perhaps Tom could play cards with you. He is really very good, I can guarantee that, even if he isn't as good as I am at gin rummy. But then, almost no one is, and if you like bridge, perhaps I could occasionally bring Laura and Tom, that is, if you would like that—"

"You're taking an awful lot of words to say you don't want to be alone with me," he said flatly, cutting through all her excuses and all her composure with that one sentence.

"It's not that—it's—" Her eyes met his and her voice froze in her throat.

"I am very well trained and housebroken, Miss Green. I promise to mind my manners in the future. If I assure you that I will keep our relationship on a strictly formal basis, will you agree to play gin with me? Or are you afraid that my card-playing will miraculously improve, and you will find that you are no longer gin rummy champion of Corver Island?"

Stacy tried to hear what he was saying above the pounding of her heart. It was all very well for him to promise to keep their relationship formal, because, of course, he could. He was in love with Dominic Rouse. Stacy couldn't possibly make him the same promise. Yet how could she explain that? Not that she wanted to explain. She would die of embarrassment if he ever guessed the way she felt about him.

After a long silence, she realized he was waiting for her answer. She murmured, "Mr. Hamilton, I—yes, of course, I will come play cards with you. I—I—I have to get back to the office now."

Why had she ever thought of herself as the cool, competent businesswoman type? As she fled to her car, she felt about thirteen years old. She had no idea how to act, speak, or think when she was near that man, even though she knew perfectly well that he had no interest in her, that he was engaged to someone else, and that he probably thought of her as what Miss Rouse would describe as "amusingly provincial." Yet somehow she must manage to remain calm during the days of visiting him and playing cards with him. She must learn to carry on friendly but impersonal conversations. He had very effectively blocked all her excuses for not spending time with him by inferring that she was afraid of his romantic advances. If she made any excuse, it would look as though she really were afraid of him. And that would definitely present her as an immature country girl.

Stacy bit her lip. She was smart, talented, and a professional decorator. She was an adult. She would not be backed into a corner by a rich, worldly-wise man. She would beat him at gin rummy, and she would also beat him at whatever other little game he was trying to play. It occurred to her that that was exactly what he was doing—playing a game with her to amuse himself through his convalescence. Was it possible? Was he that type of man? Had he intentionally kissed her at the first opportunity in order to put her in a position of embarrassment? Did he find that amusing?

Stacy's face flamed. Why hadn't she thought of that before? "All right, Mr. Smart Guy, I can play that game, too," she muttered through clenched teeth. Then she added, "That is, if I can get my stupid heart to stop pounding every time I look at you." It was not going to be easy.

Chapter Nine

Whatever game the man was playing, he didn't show any hand except his gin rummy hand. During the next week, Stacy fell into the habit of spending her evenings at Birch House. It was an easy habit to acquire. The sun was still high in the sky late into the Northwest evenings. The front and side patios of Birch House with their southwestern exposures provided delightful backgrounds for lingering.

On her first visit, Stacy only meant to stop long enough to bring Mr. Hamilton an armload of books from the Corver Island library. When he asked about the due dates or if he needed a card, she said, "No, we don't have library cards. I signed your name at the library for the books. You can keep them as long as you like."

"What do you mean, as long as I like?" he demanded.

"I mean that they have due dates in them for one month, but if you aren't finished with them all by then, keep what you want until you finish. The library won't fine you."

"Is that some special privilege to new homeowners?"

Stacy laughed. "No. It's just that what the library really wants is the return of its books when you're done with them. Some people won't return books if they owe a fine so the library quit charging fines. Now they get their books back."

"I'd love to suggest that system to a New York library," he said.

"You won't find such generosity in Seattle, either," Stacy said, "but we're more relaxed here."

"Yes, I know about the fishing."

When he saw that she was going to ignore that remark, he suggested that they have coffee on the patio. The housekeeper brought out a tray, arranged it on a table by Stacy's chair, and then disappeared into the house. She was such a quiet woman, so unlike any housekeepers that Stacy had ever known, that she asked, "Would Mrs. Enderby like to join us for coffee?"

"Mrs. Enderby is one of my hotel staff. She'd be embarrassed if you asked her."

"Do you mean that you eat by yourselves, even when there are only two of you in the house?"

Mr. Hamilton leaned back on the octagonal bench, his back against the cherry tree trunk. He gazed thoughtfully at her. "I hadn't thought it strange until you mentioned it."

"I think it is weird."

"Very well, Miss Green, tomorrow morning I shall invite Mrs. Enderby to eat breakfast with me."

"Where does she usually eat?"

"I wouldn't know. She serves me breakfast at the kitchen table unless it is nice outside. I suppose she must eat either before or after me. And now that you have done your bit about humanizing my relationship with my employee, why don't you be very kind and human and give me a chance to win a game of gin?"

As there was no polite way of refusing that invitation, Stacy said, "I'll give you a chance but you'll have to provide the skill."

And that was how the nightly gin games began. They played until dusk cut down the visibility, and Stacy had to put the cards away. Neither of them spoke much as they played. When they finished that first night, she said, "Do you need help going into the house?"

"You can help me stand up," he said. "After that, I'm fine."

Stacy caught his arm, helped him to his feet, and handed him the crutches.

"Will you be all right now?"

"You'd be surprised how efficient I am becoming on crutches, Stacy Green."

She wasn't surprised, though. As she drove home that first night, and the evenings that followed, she thought about him and found her surprise growing about a totally different subject. That he was physically strong and agile she would have guessed, and that he could adapt to swinging his weight around on crutches and figure out how to do anything for himself, she found believable. What amazed her was his disposition. He seemed happy and relaxed. She knew that Mr. Lacey came to Birch House daily, bringing all the business problems, the mail, and the messages. However, he only stayed a few hours. The rest of the day Mr. Hamilton read. Tom said that sometimes Mr. Hamilton hobbled out to the barn to watch the painting, but that much of the time he just sat on the patio, staring at the view or reading a book. He had a radio, but he hadn't even brought a portable TV with him, which he could have acquired in minutes just by asking Lacey. And yet he didn't seem to be going out of his mind at all.

When she remembered the rushed, brusque man who had popped into her office that first day, she could hardly believe that he was the same person. Gone were the neat business suits and the cold, composed expression. He wore sweaters now, and although they were beautiful cashmeres or fisherman knits, still they were sweaters. These he wore with oversize baggy pants slit up one leg to fit over the cast. Even greater than the clothing change was the change in his face. He smiled often, looked relaxed, and by the end of the week, his tan shone from the hours on the patio.

"I don't know what your leg is doing," Stacy said one evening, as she slid the cards into their box and gathered up her purse, "but the rest of you looks one hundred percent healthier. Stay around here much longer and you'll turn into another lazy Islander."

"I might even take up fishing. Just let Lacey try to find me then."

"You'd better get that cast off first."

"Oh, I don't know. It gives me a wonderful excuse. You're right, you know. I am getting lazy. Do you think your friend Tom would teach me to fish?"

"Probably. Why don't you ask him?"

"I—I don't want to impose. He might take me through some sense of duty."

"Why should he do that?" Stacy asked, surprised. "If he takes you fishing, it will be because he wants to."

"Yes, well, I am sure it is like that for you."

"Why should it be any different for you?"

He was standing in front of the French doors, a silhouette in the square of light from the house. He leaned heavily on his crutches. "Remember when you asked me to ask Mrs. Enderby to eat breakfast with me?"

"I don't remember any such thing. It was your idea," Stacy protested. "It was a very nice idea, too, and did you remember to ask her?"

"I did. She said, 'No, thank you, sir,' and that was that. I told you she would be embarrassed, and I think she was."

"Oh. Oh, my, well, Tom isn't like that."

"How can you be sure?"

"He just isn't. I know him pretty well. Anyway, right now he's probably more bored than you are, and if he could figure out a way to get you into a fishing boat with that cast, he probably would do it."

"Why is he bored?"

Stacy regretted that she had mentioned it. The story seemed so long and complicated. As she started to tell it, she could think of no way to change the subject without sounding rude.

She said, "Tom was supposed to be married this summer, but he and his girl had a fight. She's living with Laura and me because her mother takes Tom's side. And that leads to another situation. She spends every evening rehashing her woes and crying a lot and, since I have been coming up here every evening, I am leaving Laura with that load. So I am rather guilty about that."

"Ah. Fascinating. But if you didn't come here, then you would have to feel guilty about leaving poor me all alone."

"Exactly," Stacy said.

Was he smiling? It was too dark now to see. "Good,"

he continued. "Just go on feeling guiltier about me than about Laura. It's odd, though, somehow I had the idea that Tom was *your* boyfriend."

"Mine? Heavens. He's belonged to Angie since he was six years old. No, Tom is just a friend, an old friend."

"I wish you would accept me on that basis," he said slowly. Stacy stood still, her heart racing. It wasn't as though he had said anything wrong, it was just that he had touched on their relationship, and she had steeled herself to avoid the subject. She had half expected him to make a pass that first evening, thinking he was up to some sort of game, but when he remained so polite and proper she had let her guard down.

When she didn't answer, he said, "I am getting a little bored with this Miss Green–Mr. Hamilton relationship, dearie. If you are going to continue to beat me at gin every night, I should at least like us to be on first-name terms."

Stacy could have told him that she called him Avery in her dreams a thousand times a night, and that if she said his name aloud, her voice would probably break or be drowned out by her heart, but instead she said carefully, "Yes, of course."

"No lecture? No comment? What happened to the girl who used to rattle all the time?"

Stacy stepped back in the dark, bumped the small table, and overturned the tray with the coffee things. His laughter rang around her as she hurriedly picked up the pieces and placed them on the bench. She was just as glad that he was stuck on his crutches like a scarecrow on a pole and could not get down on his knees to help her.

"That is the nicest thing you've done in days," he said. "It makes me feel like the old Stacy is back with us."

"Well, really," she sputtered as she stood up and replaced the last chipped cup on the tray. "I'm glad it amuses you to hear your china breaking. There may still be bits out here but I can't see them in the dark."

"Don't worry. I'll let Mr. Lacey check in the morning. It will keep him busy."

"You're good at that, aren't you, keeping everyone busy, running them around to your tune, giving orders, manipulating people—" Stacy stopped abruptly, as though she had suddenly heard her own words. Too often her voice rattled on, uncontrolled by her brain, but usually her rattling was polite conversation to fill in gaps of silence. Suddenly, she realized that she had been saying out loud all the thoughts that she had never expressed before. These weren't the thoughts that she necessarily believed, but they were the arguments she used against her heart whenever she thought of Avery Hamilton.

"Do I manipulate you?" he said.

Stacy pressed her hands against her burning cheeks. At least, in this dim light, he could not see her blushing. "No," she whispered. "I didn't mean—I was upset about the dishes and—oh, I am so sorry."

"At least I usually know what you're thinking and that's refreshing," he said pleasantly. "Most of the people around me lie their heads off with tact and courtesy."

"I wish I could be like that, always say the right thing and not say more than I mean to and think before I speak and—oh, I don't know what's the matter with me tonight. It's getting late and I really should be leaving. Here I've kept you standing while I talk and knock over dishes, and you aren't supposed to be standing at all, are you? And listen, I really must leave, and I am sorry about the dishes, and I'm sorry about whatever I said because I didn't mean what I said, at least not the way it sounded. I think I must be tired." Her voice faded away, and she thought seriously of turning and running to her car. She knew that would be the most childish thing she could do, though, so instead, she stood quietly and waited for him to reply.

He said softly, "Good night, Stacy."

"Good night," she said, and then she fled.

It wasn't until much later that night, after she had reached home and sat through an hour of Angie's tears and Laura's pleas, that Stacy was able to think sensibly about her evening with Avery Hamilton. She wished she could tell Laura what had happened and have Laura tell her how to handle the man. Her friend could be surprisingly level headed, but with Angie around, Laura had all the "Dear Abby" duty she could manage.

When they finally dropped into their beds, Laura said, "What are we going to do, Stacy? We can't go on much longer with Angie falling apart every evening, and I don't think Angie can go on like this, either. She glues herself together for her day at work but, at this rate, she's going to come unglued soon and break into tears right there in the bank."

"I'm sorry you're getting the brunt of this. Maybe I should stay home tomorrow night and you should go play cards with Mr. Hamilton." It would be a coward's way out for both of them, though Laura couldn't know that, because Stacy wasn't sure she could face Mr. Hamilton again tomorrow.

"That's not the answer," said Laura. "I really think we need to get her together with Tom. I can't believe he knows how upset Angie is. You know Angie. She can play the little spitfire in front of people, and I bet she's never dissolved in tears with Tom."

"Do you think she would now?"

Laura sighed, then said slowly, "Stacy, I think that if Angie came face to face with Tom now, she would fall apart."

"And what would that accomplish?"

"Do you think Tom could walk away from one of her crying jags?"

Of course he couldn't. Tom was as soft hearted as Santa Claus. He was a big teddy bear and they all knew it. When Stacy said so, Laura laughed. Stacy added, "I think you're on the right track, Laura, and I think I know what to do. Tomorrow night I'll go up to Birch House after supper, and you can then notice that I've left behind some books for Mr. Hamilton. You can tell Angie that you have a client you have to see. Then, let's see, tell her you'll drop her by Birch House, and she can run in the books and take a look at the house, and you'll be back to pick her up in say, twenty minutes. Oh, I don't know, but you can think of something. Then I'll tell her, well, I'll ask her if she'll run out to the barn to get something for me while she's there and I'll have Tom in the barn."

"You'll have Tom in the barn? What are you going to do, keep him in a box?"

"No, oh, well, I'll phone him tomorrow and tell him I want him to stop by around eight to meet me to go over what he's doing. Don't worry, I'll think of something. You just get Angie up there."

"I'm willing to try anything," Laura mumbled into her pillow.

Long after Laura had drifted off to sleep, Stacy lay awake staring at the ceiling. It wasn't Tom and Angie that worried her. When it came to managing other people's lives and houses, she could be very efficient. What worried her was her own heart. It was getting totally out of control. Why had she blown up at Mr. Hamilton like that? Did he really want her to call him Avery? That wasn't much in keeping with his usual formal relations with his employees. Of course, she wasn't just an employee, was she? Wait a minute, yes, she was. She was an employee who was spending extra time with the boss because he'd had an accident about which she felt guilty. Mr. Lacey didn't even have any guilt to worry about, since the accident, he too was doing extra work, such as visiting Mr. Hamilton every morning. She knew he brought Mr. Hamilton his daily change of clothing because Mrs. Enderby had no laundry facilities at the house. Also, it wasn't her job to do the laundry. No doubt Mr. Lacey also helped him dress daily and did lots of other extra jobs. She knew that Tom, too, helped him in and out of doors during the day and did any other services he could. So she wasn't doing anything more than anyone else.

So, why, why, why, did he laugh when she dropped the tray, demand that she come by daily, trick her through her guilt feelings into keeping him company, and then refuse to be insulted when she said that he manipulated people? Why did he fluster her so much that she said such things? Was he using her to amuse himself because he couldn't find anything else that passed the time so well? Was he playing games?

Or was he simply lonely and appreciative of her company?

Stacy socked her pillow into shape, flung about in her bed, stared at the ceiling, and finally fell into a restless sleep.

The next day, true to her word, she phoned Tom from her office and caught him early, before he had started up to Birch House. "I'll be up there about eight in the evening if you could stop by then. I wanted to go over a couple of things with you," she told him.

"Sure, Stace, no problem," he said.

After she hung up, she was filled with guilt. Now she was doing exactly what she had accused Avery Hamilton of doing; she was manipulating people. Never mind that she was doing it for their own good. Suppose Angie did not fall into Tom's arms? Suppose she started screaming at him, and they had a big fight right there at Birch House? What would Mr. Hamilton think then?

Stacy closed her mind on her doubts, concentrated on the work that she had to do, and tried to ignore her aching back. Tossing all night hadn't rested her a bit. Worse, when she'd awakened in the morning, Priscilla had been sleeping on top of her stomach like a dead weight, and Stacy's spine had been uncomfortably twisted and stiff.

On the way home from the office she stopped to pick up some books for Mr. Hamilton and was careful to leave them on the couch in the apartment. During supper she talked her head off about anything at all, except possibly Mr. Hamilton or Tom. She could not quite look at Angie. Maybe their plan was a terrible mistake.

It wasn't until she was in her car and driving up Sunday Hill that Stacy realized that she was also manipulating herself. In her eagerness to help out Laura and Angie, she had arranged things so that there was no way that she could avoid going to Birch House this evening and facing Avery Hamilton.

Could she really call him "Avery"? Yet if she didn't,

he would comment on it. Who was making the rules for this game anyway?

He greeted her as though nothing had been said the previous evening, but then, he always did that. And for him, she supposed, nothing had happened. It was just for her, with her wildly beating heart, that every encounter meant something. Mrs. Enderby served their coffee on the patio, as usual, then disappeared into the house.

"I should take a walk out and see how the barn is coming," Stacy said.

"Nearly done, I think," he said. "I was out there today watching for a while."

"Tom is going to stop by this evening. I wanted to check it with him."

"What will he do when he finishes the barn?"

"I—well, I think Laura has another job he could work on, if he wants it. I'd planned for him to finish the house first, but he can't paint while you're here. You, uh, you don't know when the house will be empty?"

"I haven't made any plans. I'll probably leave the day they install the phone."

"That could be a long time," Stacy laughed.

"You did tell them I was in no hurry?"

"I told them. There's Tom's truck now." She heard it turn into the drive and head around to the barn, though she could not see it from this side of the house. She excused herself and went around to the barn, leaving Avery Hamilton alone on the octagonal bench beneath the cherry tree.

After Tom climbed out of his truck, they wandered through the barn checking the restoration. "Is there some problem?" he asked.

"No, but I am having a problem trying to budget time for this job, Tom. Obviously, you're going to finish here in a few days. I would like for us to get on with the house, but you can't do anything that would create fumes while Mr. Hamilton is in it, and I can't find out when he plans to leave."

"I don't think he knows," Tom said. "When I talk to him he acts as though he's content here. I am kind of surprised by that. Somehow I thought he was the type who would want to be in the city in the middle of things."

"I know, I thought so, too. I thought a weekend on the Island would send him rushing back to his office."

"I hope you aren't worrying about me, Stace. The house interior is really at a point where anyone can finish it if I leave."

"That's what worries me. I'm afraid you will leave. I don't want anyone else to finish the house. I want you to do the work."

"Now, Stace. I've about decided to head up to Alaska for the summer with a fishing fleet. But I won't strand you. I'll line up someone to finish this."

She didn't ask why he wanted to go to Alaska. She knew all too well. As she glanced around the barn, she realized that even if she thought of some small, puttering job to keep Tom busy this evening for an extra half an hour, she could not send Angie around the house to the barn. Angie would see Tom's truck before she ever reached the barn. For a minute Stacy wondered how she had ever talked herself into this plan. Then she glanced at Tom, saw the tightness of his jaw, and knew that if he did go to Alaska, he would only be running away from what he really wanted. Stacy steeled herself. She knew what heartache was, and she couldn't think of any reason to let it go on for Tom and Angie.

"Why don't we just stop back in the house and you can explain exactly what does need doing?" she said, turning away from the barn. In a nervous gesture she pushed the little points of dark hair back from her forehead. Her wide eyes turned away from him. Deceiving an old friend was not easy.

They went through the unfinished parlor discussing each detail of the remodeling. Stacy dragged out her questions, wondering where Angie was. Mr. Hamilton pulled himself up from the bench and swung across the patio on his crutches, to stand in the open French doors listening. When Stacy explained that Tom might be leaving for Alaska and that someone else would be taking over the job, he nodded.

And then like a lightning bolt, there was Angie, standing beside him in the open doorway, the books in her arms, her mouth open but speechless after her first shouted, "Stacy?"

"Here I am, Angie," Stacy said. From the corner of her eye she saw Tom swing around, caught the polite, curious look on Mr. Hamilton's face, and raced into an explanation to cover all the loud silences. "What a surprise! What are you doing here, Angie? Come in and see what we're doing to this place. You wouldn't recognize it, would you, or were you ever in it before? Oh, you brought those books I got for Mr. Hamilton. . . . I must have left them at home after all—how nice of you! Come in and—Tom, you show Angie what we're doing . . ." Stacy's voice faded.

Angie's small face rose, her chin jutted out, her eyes hardened. She moved into the room. It was easy for Stacy to see the determination. Angie would not back out, back down, or let it be known in any way that seeing Tom was any more important to her than seeing Stacy or Mr. Hamilton.

Tom's face had gone blank. He didn't smile and he didn't frown. He just stared at Angie as though she were some sort of apparition. Then he nodded slowly and said, "Hello, Angie."

The silence that followed was more than Stacy could bear. Finally, Angie asked, in a tight, controlled voice, how the job was coming along and Tom answered politely, very well, and did she like the wood floor? While they stared at each other and murmured senseless comments, Stacy stepped backward, then moved slowly around Angie until she was out of the French doors. In the twilight she saw that Mr. Hamilton had returned to the bench and was leaning back against the tree. He beckoned to her.

Stacy sat down beside him on the bench.

He leaned toward her and whispered to her, "Is she the reason Tom is so anxious to go to Alaska?"

Stacy nodded. He was so close she could feel his breath on her ear.

"Then may I presume that her coming here is no coincidence and that you had no real questions to ask Tom this evening?"

Stacy stared through the French doors into the lighted room. Angie and Tom were like characters on a lighted stage. Unfortunately, very little acting was going on. Both held their ground, faces polite and expressionless. Yet she realized, watching them, that neither had noticed that they were now alone together. Both were keeping up an act as though they thought they were still in the company of two outsiders.

Softly, Avery Hamilton said, "What are you, the matchmaker of Corver Island?"

Stacy turned toward him and her large eyes shone in her small pale face. "Not very successful at it, I should say."

"I've seen more subtle arranging," he teased.

"Laura and I were desperate."

"That's right. I remember you told me."

Speaking in whispers in the soft evening air created a situation that was more intimate than Stacy knew how to handle. She started to stand, felt Avery's hand on her arm, stayed where she was, glanced at him, then followed his gaze. In the lighted, empty, torn-up room behind the French doors, Angie stood shaking, her hands covering her face.

"Is that what she's been doing?" he asked.

"Every night," Stacy answered.

"That should do it," he said softly and he was right.

Tom's arms went around Angie. In the next moment, Angie was enveloped as though she were a small doll. Tom bent over her, his face pressed to the top of her head.

"If I were in better condition for it, I'd say this was the time for us to take a walk. Well, let's try, anyway," he said, and swung himself up on his crutches. He moved across the patio to the edge of the garden and stared out across the hillside to the distant water. It shone red beneath the setting sun. Stacy followed him.

"I must apologize," he added. "You seem to be a very good matchmaker."

"I didn't do much for your romance," Stacy blurted, then clapped her hands over her mouth when she realized what she had said. Avery Hamilton gazed at her, his face the flat mask that had baffled her on so many occasions. It was impossible to tell whether he was angry or amused or merely bored.

"Time will tell," he said. Stacy could not guess what that meant but neither could she find the nerve to ask him. Instead, she found herself explaining the names of the bushes in this corner of the garden. Then she identified all the places they could see across the water from the spot where they were standing.

When she finally heard Tom's truck rattle down the driveway, she said, "I really must leave now, Mr. Hamilton—"

"Avery."

"Yes." She backed into the front garden toward her car. She could barely see him now in the dusk. "Goodnight, Avery."

"Good night, Stacy."

Driving home through the moonlight, she could hear his voice saying her name. She saw him standing in the dark garden. She felt the warmth of his nearness on the bench. Long after she had said goodnight to Laura and gone to bed, Stacy lay staring at the darkness while her heart broke into a thousand pieces.

Chapter Ten

"Life is not a picture book," Stacy told herself firmly as she drove up Sunday Hill the next afternoon. True, Angie and Tom were back together again and would work out their differences now. True, Leitzel-Green Design was out of the red, thanks to the Birch House account. True, Laura was on cloud nine now that the Angie problem and the money problems were solved.

The only picture book ending that could not come true was the nonsensical one in Stacy's heart. Last night she had dreamed again of the Art Deco picture, the two faces silhouetted in front of a background of water shimmering in moonlight. One silhouette had a hard, firm chin, and the dark red of his hair shone in the moonlight. The other silhouette was less clear. At first it seemed to have perfect features and silver-blond hair. Then it changed and wavered; the chin became a bit pointed, the nose a shade too small, the hair dark.

"Dreams and picture books," she told herself sharply. "Full of nonsense. Today I am putting away all that childish nonsense. I am going up to the house to make one last check of what needs to be done, and then I am telling Mr. Hamilton firmly that the restoration will be completed when he has moved out. In the meantime, he can jolly well invite his staff, his relatives, his business associates, or anyone else he cares to if he wishes to be entertained. Stacy Green is retiring from the job of social director at Birch House."

When she turned into the driveway, she discovered that she might not have to give her little speech after all. Her problem had been solved. Dominic Rouse stood in the open doorway, and called out a polite good afternoon.

"How nice that you're back," Stacy said as she walked to the house.

"Come around on the side patio," Miss Rouse said. "I am glad you stopped by today. We need to settle things quickly, and I know you will be a great help."

Stacy followed her around to the side of the house where she had spent the last week under the cherry tree watching the sunsets. Now the sun was high in the sky, and Avery was in his favorite spot on the octagonal bench.

"Oh, look who's here," he said pleasantly. "You're a bit early, aren't you?"

"I—I thought I would come up this afternoon because I was on my way somewhere else, and Birch House was on the way, and I wanted to ask you—tell you—discuss a few things. But it isn't important right now. I can come back later."

"Stay," he said, stretching a hand toward her. "Dominic, Stacy has been my salvation this past week. She's kept me supplied with books, magazines, and a gin rummy partner."

Miss Rouse smiled her angel smile. She brushed an invisible piece of lint from her linen suit, then said slowly, "Miss Green, I know you are anxious to complete this job. The contractor, too, must be inconvenienced by the delay. I realize you cannot do another thing with Avery in the house. I do wish you would tell him so firmly. He doesn't believe me."

Mr. Hamilton told her that he was in no particular hurry about the restoration. Miss Rouse explained carefully that the house could not be left half-finished. Their voices were low, controlled, polite, yet what they said could just as well have been screamed. Stacy watched in fascination as Miss Rouse pointed out that the contractors would leave and there would be no workmen. Mr. Hamilton stated that he was sure that workmen could be found at any time. He added that since there was no deadline on the job, he could not see why she cared.

And then he said, "Or is there some deadline? Have you given *Homes of Distinction* a date to photograph Birch House?"

He said it so quietly that he could have been asking the time of day. Yet the words had the effect of a bomb blast. Miss Rouse went pale. Stacy realized that Miss Rouse had never told him about the magazine layout plans. Although he had learned of the plans from Stacy on the day they went to the auction show-room in Tacoma, he had obviously never mentioned to Miss Rouse that he knew.

Miss Rouse said, "No, and to tell you the truth, Avery, I have lost interest in this project. I wonder now if the best thing might be to put Birch House up for sale."

He raised his eyebrows slightly. Otherwise his face remained a mask. "You do change your mind easily, Dominic. First you canceled the wedding, now you plan to unload Birch House. Tell me, love, what next?"

"I didn't cancel anything. I merely *postponed* our wedding. But I am admitting now that I made a mistake about Birch House. You did buy it for me, didn't you, and now I don't want it. It's been a jinx. If you hadn't bought it you wouldn't have broken your leg, and we could have been married on the date we had planned."

As Stacy watched these two handsome people who somehow resembled all the perfect couples in wedding illustrations, she knew that she must tell Miss Rouse the truth. If she were fired off the job now, it didn't matter. Tom would still finish the painting. The design firm was solvent. Phillips would keep his contract. All that would be lost was her own pride, and she deserved to lose that. She realized in a flash that she had let her heart rule her head. She had wanted to please him, be near him, see him as often as possible, even though she knew he would never be interested in her, knew he belonged to someone else. Her heart had tricked her. Now she would have to stop listening to its pounding. She would have to tell the truth. It would be better for everyone, even for herself, because then she would be out of his life forever. She could go off in a corner and die of a broken heart. It would all be done with quickly, which was far better than this slow suffering.

She said, "Miss Rouse, it isn't Mr. Hamilton's fault and it isn't the fault of Birch House. I don't know why I didn't tell you when it happened. I guess I was too upset."

She heard Avery's low voice telling her to be still. She heard her own voice rising to a high, nervous squeak that she hated but could not control, as she said, "I knocked him down the stairs. I hit him with a light fixture. I mean, I didn't do it on purpose, but just the same, I did it."

The silence that followed seemed to echo with her voice. Stacy clamped her mouth shut and tightened the muscles of her jaw. If she tried to say another word, she might burst into tears and she did not want to do that.

Miss Rouse finally said, "Is that true?" to Mr. Hamilton, and he nodded. Was he smiling? Stacy looked away from him. Really, he was too much. He would drive her mad.

"And you kept her on the job?" Miss Rouse said. "Why?"

He said firmly, "Because she is the best gin rummy player I have ever met."

"What?" To Stacy's surprise, this time Miss Rouse had shrieked.

"She is also a very good decorator, which is what I hired her for."

Miss Rouse swung toward Stacy, her eyes blazing. "Do you know what you've done? You changed all my wedding plans, canceled the honeymoon trip to Europe—"

"Stacy didn't change anything," Avery cut in. "You did. You're the one who postponed the wedding, Dominic. It was your decision. I was willing to go through with the wedding. We could have gone to Europe."

"With you in a cast?" she sputtered.

"Ah, no," he said softly, but his voice was ice, "that would not have looked well in the wedding photos, would it, my dear?"

"No, it wouldn't," she snapped, "but as soon as you get that thing off I will arrange the wedding, you know that."

He didn't smile or frown or raise his voice. He just said quietly, "I don't want you to go to all that trouble, Dominic."

Stacy wished the earth would open up beneath her feet and swallow her whole. This was not a scene that anyone could watch and enjoy. Yet she knew there was nothing she could say or do. Meanwhile, Dominic stared, speechless, then turned and walked to her car, her back rigid. It seemed like hours to Stacy before the car backed out of the drive and wound down the hill.

"I could use a cup of coffee," Avery said.

"Oh!" Stacy jerked around, startled, her mind still in a whirl from Miss Rouse's departure. "Shall—shall I call Mrs. Enderby?"

"Mrs. Enderby is in town running errands. Do you suppose you could manage to put together a pot of coffee?"

Thankful for any excuse to move away from the spot to which she had felt rooted, Stacy hurried into the house. For a brief moment she had thought of apologizing to him for causing such an uproar. If she had not mentioned the accident, Dominic would not have been so annoyed and none of this would have happened. Then it occurred to her that he was a man who made things happen his own way, and if he decided that he wanted Miss Rouse back, he would find his own answers. Besides, no matter how guilty she felt, she could not say that she was sorry to him one more time. He had told her to stop apologizing and she was beginning to understand why. If she made errors, it did not correct them to apologize. What she had to do was stop causing problems.

With all her confused thoughts tumbling through her mind, Stacy managed to find the teakettle, fill it with water, put it on to boil, measure coffee into the pot, and find cups. The pot whistled.

"It's boiling," he said, "and that relieves my mind."

She whirled around and saw him leaning against the kitchen doorway, his crutches supporting most of his weight.

"Why is that?" she asked.

"At least I know you can boil water."

"That's not nice," she sputtered.

"No, and it isn't fair," he admitted. "You can do many things, Stacy Green. Anyone can make a meal in a kitchen but it takes a real talent to create a kitchen. I'm pleased with this one."

"You picked the stove, and that really sets the tone for this room," she said, nodding toward the wood stove with its green ceramic tiles. "About Miss Rouse, I think she was a bit upset—"

"A bit upset?"

"By what I said, and I know I promised not to tell her and I also promised not to apologize so I won't say any more about that—"

"That's something to be thankful for—"

"But I do think that after she cools down a bit she'll regret her anger, and when you have that awful cast off your leg you'll feel more like your old self—"

"What is it you're trying to say?"

Stacy continued, "And if it would help any if I wrote her a note, then I would be more than happy to do that. I mean, I don't want to be the cause of—well, of any trouble between the two of you."

"What sort of trouble?"

"Oh—uh, well, your wedding postponement—" Her voice faltered.

"The wedding isn't postponed. It is canceled. I understood that. Dominic understood it. Where were you?"

Stacy poured the boiling water into the coffeepot. Then she looked up at him. "You didn't mean it, did you?" she said. "You were angry. But you won't call off your wedding and sell Birch House and give up everything just because of a few angry words?"

"Ah. The matchmaker of Corver Island is at it again."

She arranged the coffeepot and cups on the round oak table. The housekeeper had placed a large bowl of daisies in the center of the old linen tablecloth. It truly was a beautiful room, Stacy thought. She might even enjoy cooking in this kitchen.

"It would be a shame to sell Birch House," she said. "You could spend years trying to find an equally nice piece of property. Even if Miss Rouse doesn't want it now, maybe in the future she will change her mind."

"No doubt Miss Rouse will change her mind about many things, but not about Birch House."

"Is she that upset?" Stacy asked in a small voice.

"That has nothing to do with it. Birch House belongs to me and I intend to keep it."

Stacy sighed with relief.

"Does that please you?" he asked, surprised.

"Yes. I wouldn't want just anyone to buy Birch House. Someone else might not appreciate it. I've watched you on the patio and I've seen you looking at the view. I know it means something to you. It's a special house, really, it shouldn't go to just anyone—"

"It isn't going to just anyone. I am going to give it to someone."

Her eyes widened in her face until they were large dark circles. "I thought you said—"

"I said I wasn't going to sell Birch House."

"But then—I thought you'd already given it to Miss Rouse."

"Ah, it was to be a wedding present. I think wedding presents usually get canceled right along with the weddings, don't they? Besides, she definitely does not want Birch House."

"Maybe not," Stacy admitted, "but I expect she still wants you."

"I think you just failed at matchmaking," he said slowly. "Open your eyes, Stacy Green. Dominic never wanted me. She wanted to marry my family name, my social position, and whatever else went with that. She wanted an elaborate wedding that could be written up in all the society pages. She wanted a lifetime of invitations to the right places, and mentions in the right publications. Underneath all that, I don't think she ever wanted me."

"I can't believe that."

"No? Why not?"

"Because—because—" Stacy hesitated, took a breath and rushed in, knowing she would later regret it but unable to stop her mouth. "Because I—you—she loved you, surely, and you love her, and you've had a quarrel. But those don't last, and I think you were hasty when you told her to cancel the wedding, and I think she was shocked to hear you say it—anyone would be. But, if you tell her you didn't mean it, I think she'll probably fall into your arms like—like—oh, I don't know."

"I don't want her in my arms," he said flatly. "You are a very talented decorator and a wickedly clever card player, but when it comes to love, you have a few blind spots."

Stacy decided that she had said enough. She picked up the coffeepot and filled the cups, taking her time. It kept her hands busy and saved her from having to look at him. He swung into the room on his crutches and stood beside her at the table.

"First of all," he said, his mouth so close that she could feel his breath on her ear, "I am not in love with Dominic. Second, I don't think I ever was."

Stacy couldn't keep quiet after a statement like that. "Then why did you plan to marry her?"

"Probably for the same empty reasons she planned to marry me. We have mutual friends, associates, social circles, a lot of dumb reasons. Also I had never been in love, so how could I know? Also, I had never had anyone in love with me, so I didn't know what that was like, either."

"Do you expect me to believe that?" Stacy said.

"I'm not especially loveable, although I am working on it."

Was he laughing at her again? Annoyed, Stacy said,

"You've probably had dozens of women in love with you. I don't see how you could help it."

"Let's skip the dozens and get down to specifics. What about you?" he asked.

Stacy jumped as though she had received an electric shock. She swung around, bumped him with the coffee-pot, and watched in horror as steam rose from the pants leg that was now soaked with coffee. With a scream she ran to the sink, grabbed a towel, soaked it in cold water, rushed back to him, and knelt in front of him, dabbing wildly at the wet, steaming material.

She heard herself stammering apologies, exclamations, and even some swear words she had forgotten she knew. When her thoughts finally caught up with her actions, she glanced up. He was leaning forward on his crutches, looking down at her, and he had the most fiendish smile Stacy had ever seen on such a nice face.

"Aren't you burned? Doesn't it hurt?" she cried.

"Fortunately, you pushed me downstairs a couple of weeks ago and broke my leg, so now I have a cast on it, and no, my cast is not in pain."

Stacy stood up slowly and backed away from him. She had been so worried, so horrified, and there he was, laughing at her. She knew from the trembling that shook her whole frame that she would burst into tears if he said one more word. Fierce anger surged through her. She jutted out her lip.

"I don't know what kind of games you think you're playing," she cried, "but I am tired of them. I came up here today to tell you that the workmen can finish the job whenever you want them to. They don't need me anymore; they know what to do, and, as of this very minute, I am resigning from this job. If you need anything more from my office, Laura will come up and help you and—"

"Shut up!" he snapped.

Stacy's eyes blinked with shock.

For the first time since she'd met him, his face was twisted with emotion, but Stacy couldn't tell what sort of emotion. Was he angry, sad, amused, hysterical?

He shouted, "Talk about games, you're the one who

has poured wine and coffee on me, fallen off a ladder on me, knocked me downstairs, broken my dishes, tried to burn my hide off, and cared enough about me to come running when I needed you. You are a weird combination of characteristics, Stacy Green, and it is going to take me a lifetime to sort them out."

She started to protest but he outshouted her. "I love you, don't you know that?"

Then Stacy did cry. She stood in the middle of the kitchen staring at him, her black eyes shining with tears. The tears were running slowly down her face, and she couldn't even raise her hand to brush them away. He moved over to her, wrapped his arms around her, and dropped one of his crutches. Stacy clung to him to keep him from falling and also because it made her feel better to cling to him. She buried her wet face in his sweater.

"I am asking you to share my life with me," he said softly. "Also, anything else you want. I would give you Birch House, but then, I can't, can I, because it is yours already whether you marry me or not."

She lifted her face to look at him. "I—I don't understand."

"This house was nothing but an abandoned wreck when I bought it. You've put yourself into it and made it charming. It really is yours. I haven't any use for it. Of course, if you'd like to share it with me, I'd like that."

Stacy smiled. "Is that a proposal?"

"I think I proposed a few minutes ago," he said.

Stacy said, "I love you, too."

"Is that an answer?"

"It should be."

When he stopped kissing her, he said, "Do you think Phillips and Tom can finish this job while we're off on a honeymoon trip?"

"They'd be delighted. We were all beginning to think we could never get you out of this house."

"I only stayed here to be near you."

Stacy retrieved his crutch, tucked it under his arm, and stepped away from him. She tried to give him a firm, no-nonsense look. "That's not true. You were still in love with Miss Rouse."

"I was still engaged to Miss Rouse. I was never in love with Miss Rouse. For your information, I made up my mind when I was lying in the hospital that I would come stay here until I figured out some way to detach myself from Dominic and attach myself to you."

"You what?" Stacy squeaked.

"I think it started when you fell on top of me after you broke my leg. Later, when I was lying in the hospital, I remembered the way you looked at me while you were waiting for the ambulance. The look on your face was—to tell you the truth, Stacy, when I thought about it, I realized that you were looking at me as though you could die of shock, and what's more, as though you loved me."

"What! I never!"

"I know," he laughed. "I didn't figure you knew you loved me. That's why I decided to stay here until you found it out for yourself."

"That's about the most conceited thing—"

"Don't say it," he whispered. He caught her hand and pulled her back into his arms. Against her mouth, he said softly, "I think we both fell in love at the same time. It just took you longer to admit it because you're so stubborn."

She would have told him what she thought of that idea if he hadn't closed her mouth with a kiss. By the time he raised his face from hers, she had forgotten what she was going to say.